Whines & Spirits

John A Connor

John A Connor
Whines & Spirits
This edition published in 2019 by
Chalkway Graphics
Haben
West Sussex
The right of John Connor to be identified as
the author of the work has been asserted by him
in accordance with the
Copyright, Design & Patents Act 1988.
All rights reserved. No part of this publication may be
produced in any form or by any means - graphic,
electronic or mechanical including photocopying,
recording, taping or information storage and retrieval
systems – without the prior permission, in writing,
of the publisher.
Cover designed by Chalkway Graphics.

Also by John A Connor and available from Amazon Kindle

SPECULATIVE FICTION

Short Circuits

The late **Sir Patrick Moore**, Astronomer and TV Presenter
described **Short Circuits**, John A Connor's first collection of stories as:
"A very lively and entertaining little book.
When you read it, you will find something to really appeal to you.
I am sure you will enjoy reading it as much as I did."

Fifty Percent of Infinity

Twenty more, thought provoking tales from the world just around the corner: a world that may or may not be our own. Temporal overlaps; imagined realities; alien cooking.

Seventeen Times as High as the Moon

Everything from extra-terrestrial encounters to temporal displacement; talking fridges to intergalactic song contests. Even people who think they don't like science fiction, like this science fiction!

Sixty Second Eternity

What happens when you unravel the bonds between reality and possibility? Where do you find yourself if you set off for the edge of the universe – and keep going? And, if we can't record events, can we be sure that they ever really happened?

HUMOROUS

Puck's Hassle

"An inconsequential community, a little north west of the previous junction. Comprises one public house, The Stoat and Gaiter and little of further interest. History: undistinguished, although there is some possibility that in previous centuries the town may have possessed an apostrophe."

Take a trip down the sideroads of your imagination and discover that Jakarta's neckline isn't the only thing going down in the elusive village of Puck's Hassle.

with thanks to Andrew, Bob,
David, Don, Mike and Wendy
for their advice
and encouragement

John A Connor was born in Petworth,
West Sussex, England,
attended the old Midhurst Grammar School,
trained in graphic design at
the West Sussex College of Art in Worthing
and went on to a career with the provincial press.
He has had numerous stories and articles published
and was the illustrator of a sci-fi comic strip
which ran for a record-breaking
twenty-nine years.

CONTENTS

Grave Concern 1
Endless Flight 7
Proof of Existence 11
Empty Promises 17
Hereafter 25
The Bottom of the Garden 29
Turn for the Worse 37
Our Kind 41
Against the Grain 43
Starfighter 51
The Rat 55
Ring in the New 57
Future Plans 63
Entombed 69
Countless times 73
Through a Glass, Darkly 85
Mortal, Invisible 89
Just Desserts 95
The Hand 99
Night Shift 107
The House in the Wood 115
The Sexton 123

Grave concerns

Two bloody hours! Barlow thumbed the disconnect button of his mobile and thumped petulantly at the steering wheel of his car. That was *one* motoring organisation that wouldn't be seeing any more of his money. Two freaking hours! Didn't they realise he was stuck out here in the middle of nowhere at three in the morning? Well yes, they did – because he had just told them in a manner that couldn't have made his situation any clearer. And what had that stupid cow on the other end of the line said? *We're experiencing heavier than usual demands for our services so there may be some delay in responding to your request!* He shook his clenched fists in frustrated anger and thumped the wheel again, more violently.

Useless effing car! Why, oh, why hadn't he stayed on the motorway? At least he might have made it to the next service station. Instead, when the electrics had started to play up, he'd made that idiotic decision to cut across country in the belief that if the lights failed completely, he'd be able to keep driving without fear of some brainless cop pulling him over. In the event, when the inevitable did happen and he was plunged into near total darkness on an unlit lane, he had panicked, hit the brakes and stalled the engine; following which, he had discovered the vehicle to be completely lifeless. No ignition, no heater and, unsurprisingly, no lights.

Barlow shivered and sought the reassuring glow of the mobile phone's display screen. He didn't like the dark. He never had, not since he was a child. No doubt there had been some incident, buried now in his subconscious, which had heightened his fear. Maybe he had been shut in a cupboard, locked in a shed; he had no idea. He'd tried to rationalise it. Had forced himself to climb the unlit stairs of his parents' old house, telling himself that there was nothing lying in wait in the velvety blackness beyond the bend; but he'd never made it to the top step before fear had gripped him and he'd run back and snapped on the light.

Of course, Stella, his bitch of a wife, had never understood. She'd treated the whole thing as one big joke, right from their first night together when he'd insisted on leaving that small gap in the curtains. And after she'd uncovered his weakness, she'd taken every opportunity to play on it. Of course, there had been plenty of other things, other points of disagreement, other examples of their utter incompatibility but it had been that moment with the curtains and her raucous laughter that had, so to speak, been the first nail in her coffin.

Despite the dark and the cold, Barlow smiled for a moment, then he sat back and considered his situation. He was in a black car, stuck on a bend in the lane, on a moonless night – it was a recipe for disaster. He'd be safer waiting off-road somewhere and since the heater was kaput, the only benefit his vehicle had to offer was a comfortable seat. Well, he'd been driving for two hours, and sitting for two more whilst he awaited the breakdown services, held no special appeal, so he opened the door cautiously, listened for approaching engine sounds, and climbed stiffly out into the night.

In some curious manner, despite the dark, the world seemed to expand around him, stretching off invisibly in all directions. Somewhere, way off to his right, a dog barked briefly but otherwise there was silence. He shivered again, this time not from the cold but from a rising trepidation and turning, he circled his car, one hand brushing its bodywork, and headed for the unseen verge, finding it only by shuffling his feet along the tarmac and into the grass. Cursing, he took out his mobile again and thumbed the buttons. The screen lit and threw the faintest of illumination onto the scene before him. High, dense hedges, punctuated just where he stood by a small gate, decoratively carved and varnished. A garden maybe? Whatever, it seemed to offer some sanctuary from the roadway and he pushed his way in and stepped onto a gravel path.

The phone chimed, indicating that its battery was low, as he held it out before him like a talisman offering protection from unseen dangers. It revealed nothing but darkness. If the path led to a house, there was no sign of a reassuring light. He took a few more steps and glimpsed a rectangular

Grave concerns

shape to one side of the track. He stepped nearer and held the phone close. It was a signboard announcing, in gothic capitals that this was 'Mayfield Cemetery'.

Barlow swallowed, hard. Finding himself in a cemetery might, under present circumstances, have been sufficient to speed his pulse but that it should be this very graveyard was more unnerving even than the blanketing darkness. He felt his way back to the gravel and, guiding himself slowly by the sound of it beneath his shoes, he made his way into the centre where, he remembered, a giant yew stood marking a crossing of paths. He found the tree by stumbling into it and stretching out his arm swung the phone in a slow arc until its light traced, dimly, the shape of a figure, raised hands, wings of feathered stone. He crossed to the angel and moved past it, holding his makeshift torch low to the ground, examining the engraved markers lining the path. He was confused at first by a high mound of loose earth, close to the path's edge, where he thought to find the plot but he saw, as he ran the pale light over it, that it was the spoil from a newly dug grave, carefully piled onto a wide strip of tarpaulin which ran over the lip of the excavation. What he sought was close beside the fresh soil.

Stella had grown up in the village; as far as he knew, her parents still lived there. That was why their daughter had returned to it after the accident - because that was what everyone accepted it had been: an accident.

At the time, Barlow had been filled with

trepidation as his anger subsided and he realised the implications of his actions. He had stood there, immobile, looking down the stairway at her lifeless body, the limbs arranged at unlikely angles, and he had, momentarily, deeply regretted his actions. But then he'd pulled himself together, called for an ambulance and, from there on, things had progressed in a satisfactory manner without his role being called into question; no one doubting that he was the grieving widower.

Bending down, his fingers traced the outline of the deeply incised letters. "In loving memory. Stella Barstow." What on earth had compelled him to come here, tonight of all nights, the anniversary of her...death? What strange twists of fate had immobilised his car and lured him to this, her final resting place. For a moment he imagined her, in her coffin, arms and legs awry in gruesome parody of her moment of demise. He shivered for the third time that evening and stood determinedly, pointing the mobile towards his feet to light his step back from the graveside.

'Stupid bitch!' he said loudly, speaking to the unhearing dead all around him and, as his words were swallowed up by the night, his phone chimed one final time and switched itself off, leaving him in utter darkness. As he balanced there, one foot already lifted in the action of leaving, something moved through the cemetery and brushed an unfolding wing across his face. He screamed, trod back onto a surface slick and steeply angled and, as his feet lost purchase, fell, his chest impacting

Grave concerns

sickeningly with the wet tarpaulin where it crossed the edge of the cut turf. He threw out a desperately clutching hand, his fingers locking around a rough tear in the thick material. For a long second he swung, pain stabbing through his shoulder as the fabric sheet lost traction with the wet clay and began sliding into the rectangular pit, carrying with it the excavated soil. He hit the bottom of the grave with a thump, the earth pouring down, covering his face, stifling his breath and committing him to the most complete darkness he would ever know. And he understood, in that instant, that his lifetime's fear had not been the consequence of some forgotten, early trauma but had been a foretelling of what was to come.

As the wide, open world of the night shrank in and encased him, he thought he heard, from somewhere very close at hand, the sound of raucous laughter.

Endless flight

Henderson brought the Camel in low over the wheat fields, hopelessly seeking the double line of poplars edging the road, as a guide to the location of the landing strip. He pushed lightly on the stick, correcting the aircraft's tendency to lift from level flight and scanned the terrain for a familiar landmark.

He fingered the small, silver pendant at his neck, an amulet to guard against his death: Chloe's gift at their last meeting in Sussex, when they had walked the beagles on the high hills and looked down on the blue-green world as she gripped his hand and they imagined that they were *both* pilots, soaring together above the wooded valleys and idle, twisting river; and believing that their journey together could go on forever and that they would never need to touch the ground again.

Far off to the east, a diagonal smear across the clean, October sky acted as a marker to a lost life and showed where the aerial battle, which he had so recently observed, still raged.

Now, in his open cockpit, there was no sound of the conflict, and the movement of the warm breeze, which would once have been amplified to a roar by the headlong passage of the plane's plywood and fabric superstructure, was absent too.

Endless flight

Chloe had died when the stick of incendiaries turned the hotel to flame and Henderson had stood across the street, where he had gone for cigarettes, and watched the fire. Later, he had watched too as her husband raged impotently against both her infidelity and her death and cursed to hell the man who had brought her there.

Which it might have been, curse or charm, which preserved Henderson when the Fokker's shells shredded his cockpit and ripped through his body, he did not know. There had been a brief moment of unendurable pain and then another of transition, before he had found himself whole again, his hand unbloodied on the joystick, the camel cruising silently through the smoke and flame of the war.

Henderson had followed that long, tapering column of oily smoke, spiralling down and around it until he could see the cratered earth and the shattered wreckage where the Spitfire had impacted with the golden, autumnal farmland. Then he had pulled up and let the rotary engine help him into a tight, clockwise turn, back towards the lost airfield, which he no longer thought to find; in two decades it had eluded his search as he flew on and on in his aerial limbo.

The new fighters were sleek, single-winged and fast as a falcon but he could tell from the insignia that the combatants were the same; their brief tumbling descent from the light, bright firmament to empty, dark oblivion, just as final.

For too few years the faded world had lay at peace; the pockmarked fields smoothed and planted; the burned and splintered tree-trunks cleared for new woodlands, the poison drained from the tired land. Now, tanks crawled anew over the carefully tended crops, columns of men marched again through the rebuilt towns and the children of long dead friends fell to their own deaths from the same unforgiving skies.

Once, he had lied to secure a night of love; men had burned in the battle he'd foresworn and somehow that illicit, selfish act had condemned him, in penance, to this endless sortie. For the ten thousandth time he turned for home and the colour-drained countryside slipped away below him, eluding identification, forbidding contact, as he flew into his endless tomorrow.

Proof of existence

The stone had stood high on the flanks of the moor for a thousand years: a giant slab of granite thrusting up from among the heather and providing a way-marker for uncertain travellers on the valley path far below. But though many had been grateful for its guidance when the track was lost beneath the snow or when wildfire had scoured the heath of a clear way, few would take the route to the summit, under the monolith's long black shadow, for legend told that the stone marked an ancient grave and that the spirit from that tomb walked the mountain at night: a fearsome, headless warrior that spelled doom to any who saw it. Daniel was sure that all these tales were nonsense, fuelled by superstition and a flagon or two of the fiery, local spirit. After all, he argued, with anyone who would listen, these were times of knowledge and enlightenment; machines had been made for the printing of books; new lands had been discovered far across the oceans; in the cities great clocks told not only the hour of the day but the rising of the moon in its quarters. It was time to put away a fear of the dark and a belief in goblins and examine the world around them in a new way.

'You should be careful of what you say,' said his brother, nervously, 'there are matters about which we know little. Only last month the peddler from

Proof of existence

Ickford told how a child had been taken by the headless ghost. How the hillside opened and swallowed them both down.'

'Ha! Old 'Torncoat' Tom? He's drunk more often than he's sober and his tales help sales of his amulets and potions. There is no headless ghoul on the hill and no grave either! The stone's just a stone; an outcrop like any other. I'll prove it to you, Charles. I'll take a spade and I'll dig my way around the stone and if I find a burial, I'll give you half the inheritance I'll receive as your elder brother! But don't grow too avaricious, for there's nothing but soil and rocks on the top, as you will see!'

Daniel was as good as his word, since the anticipation of a small fortune gave him the leisure to indulge his claim, and he took two of the gardeners and had them clear the space about the stone, although they would not start within an hour of dawn nor stay at the approach of dusk, even though their future tenure rested on their compliance with their master's wishes. So, when they were done, Daniel dismissed them back to their vegetables and began to dig alone.

Each summer's day he would trek up to the summit and excavate a new area of the moor and each evening he would return to mock his brother's continued anxiety at his activities. At last, when it was clear to him that no grave was to be found and yet still his sibling clung to the validity of the old story, he announced that he would spend a night by the stone and that his survival would be confirmation of his own claims. His brother begged

Whines & spirits

him earnestly to reconsider his plan but Daniel laughed at his concern and that evening he struck out with a pack of provisions and a blanket roll.

Neither his brother nor any other living soul ever saw him again.

Next morning when the sun had risen high in the sky and Daniel had not returned, Charles summoned the two gardeners and set off in trepidation for the fell but when they crossed the shoulder of the hill all three stopped dead in their tracks and let out a cry of horror.

The stone was gone! The hilltop was outlined smooth and empty against the clear sky. None of them dared go further to discover Daniel's fate. They returned to the village and word of what they had found spread and not one of that generation ever climbed the fell again.

Three hundred years passed and Daniel and Charles' descendants still lived in the village beneath the ridge, although by now it had become a small town. It happened that one of their number, also named Daniel, took up the study of history and that one July, when they were all gathered together to celebrate his birthday, his mother produced a trunk filled with documents which she told him charted much of the family's past. A delighted Daniel rummaged through the contents and came across a diary kept by his namesake centuries before and in this way he came to learn of the search for the interred warrior and of the legend that

Proof of existence

surrounded him. The last few pages of the diary had been completed by another hand and told of the conclusion to Daniel's search and of the vanished stone.

'Oh come on, Harry!' exclaimed Daniel, as he and his own brother examined the document, 'we must have some of this, old bean! I mean, it's not every day you encounter tales of headless horsemen and disappearing dolmens in your own family, eh?'

'Headless he may have been,' replied his brother, dryly, 'but I see no mention of equine interests. Get your facts right Dan, do.'

'Right, no horses but still plenty of mystery don't y'think? What happened to cousin Danny do you imagine?'

'Not cousin, broth, more like a many times great grandfather, but obviously we've got to investigate, agreed?'

'Sure thing!' Daniel grinned enthusiastically. 'The gals are off to town, what say we make a start tomorrow?'

The brothers arrived at the summit in the heat of the midday sun having woken late and breakfasted well, and they were hot and not a little out of breath from their exertions but they soon forgot their discomfort when they made their first discovery.

Harry had been prodding the end of his shooting stick into the turf and after a while he let out a grunt and began to move more methodically over the ground.

'Why, I believe I've found the stone!' he called, after a minute or two, 'it's an inch or three under the

Whines & spirits

topsoil. It's just fallen over, simple as that! All that fuss for nothing. What a rum do!'

Now, the brothers had one thing in common with their long gone predecessor, they too had the funds necessary to indulge their passions; and so, once they had decided that it would be amusing to re-erect the stone there was little obstacle to their executing the procedure – although the work required considerably more effort and expense than anyone could have foreseen. To wit, a gang of eight workmen, a twenty-foot 'A' frame and a generous donation to the local rugby club Christmas fund.

As the massive slab finally inched its way back to the vertical, a shriek went up from the ladies present, who had gathered to witness the culmination of all this planning. Under the slab, impressed into the sandy surface, was the unmistakable outline of a spread-eagled skeleton.

'Well,' said Daniel, after the ladies had been comforted and led away for reviving cups of tea, 'now we know what happened to poor old Danny. All that digging round the bottom of the stone must have weakened the supporting ground and the damn thing keeled over and flattened him.'

'Mmm,' concurred his brother, temporarily incommoded by the act of lighting his pipe, 'but the odd thing,' and here he paused to draw the tobacco into life, 'the really odd thing, old bean, is... why doesn't he have a head?'

Empty promises

I knew it was going to be a bad day as soon as I took the call from Max.

'What the hell do *you* want?' I barked, before he'd had chance to utter a word, 'because in case it's escaped your attention, I'm trying to edit a magazine here and I've got a deadline in three days' time. You know what deadlines are, don't you? You've missed them often enough!'

'Hey! Jack, come on,' whined the voice on the other end of the phone, 'don't be like that, I've got a story for you.'

'A story!' it was all I could do to stop myself from throwing the instrument through the office window. 'You want me to tell you where you can stuff it, pal?'

'No, listen, please! I know I let you down a couple of times but I had problems...'

'You had problems?' I roared, 'YOU had problems! What about my problems, you useless ...' I groped for a suitable Anglo-Saxon epithet and gave Max an opportunity to interrupt.

'Jack, please, I think I might be on to something big.'

That was where I hung up. I'd heard the same thing from Max a hundred times and it seemed that just as often, he'd failed to deliver the goods and left me to patch the holes in my editorial. Oh, he was a

Empty promises

good enough journalist – no, strike that out – he was a brilliant journalist, when he could be persuaded to get off his scrawny backside and do some work. Unfortunately, those occasions only arose when there was a 'Z' in the month and the moon was pink. The rest of the time he spent propping up the bar at Angelo's and dreaming up ways to become a world-famous author without expending too much energy.

I was still calming down when Mike, my deputy, came in and threw a sheaf of documents onto my desk.

'It's Armageddon!' he announced, misplacing his references as usual. 'Bloody disaster! That,' and he pointed to the offending file of paperwork, 'is an injunction, sent via Harcourt and Haribone, the London solicitors acting on behalf of Magnam Press, forbidding the publication of our leading feature on the grounds of copyright infringement.'

'What!' I wailed, grabbing up the top sheet and scanning it despairingly. 'Have you called...'

'Harry Forbes? Yes, and he says it's unbreakable but he's working on it.'

'And...?'

'Four days, minimum...'

'Four days! We go to press in three!'

'I know, I know - and Harry says don't hold your breath anyway. Look Jack, it seems the whole article was lifted word for word from a piece that Magnam ran three years ago. Obviously, we can sue McKenzie but whether he's got the money is...'

Whines & spirits

'Beside the bloody point!' I said, screwing the legal transcript into a ball and hurling it into the waste bin. 'We haven't got a lead article and the press is ready to roll on Friday morning.'

'What about using that story we spiked last month, the one on the search for a dinosaur in the Congo?'

'It was a hoax, they had the exposition in The Star, remember?'

'We could set up an interview with that woman in Swindon who was abducted by Uranians?'

'She's in Broadmoor, and besides, you're forgetting the whole point of the exercise. *I Can Scarcely Believe It!* specialises in stuff that's oddball and off the wall and next month we're supposed to hit the news-stands for Hallowe'en. We've been trailing our *Haunted Britain Special* since June; we can't just switch to bloody aliens, we'll be the laughing stock of the magazine trade. It'll destroy our sales and kill our ad revenue. We've got to lead with something about the supernatural or I'll be back working for Macramé Monthly. Now, think, who the hell do we know who specialises in ghosts and ghoulies? Oh, no, no, not...'

'Max? It's his field, after all.'

'No! I will not have Max Warnstone writing for this magazine again.'

'Well, technically, he never has written for this magazine – he's never got his stuff in on time.'

'Exactly!'

'But we're desperate and he may be working on something.'

Empty promises

'He is – I just told him where to insert it – a couple of minutes before you came in.' I stared defiantly at Mike and he looked back pleadingly at me and I swore, grabbed my coat and set off for Max's rooms, across the street.

'Hello Jack!' There was no disguising the expression on Max's face as he waved me into his dingy bed-sit. It was a mixture of anticipation, relief and smug satisfaction and I could see that there was no point in pretending that my generous nature had persuaded me to give him one last chance, a gambit that I had been rehearsing on my way over. I decided to come clean.

'I'll cut straight to the chase,' I told him. 'I wouldn't rely on you to write a birthday card for your own mother but I'm desperate. We've got a legal problem with next month's main story and there are just forty-eight hours to find a replacement. You told me this morning that you had something big. Can you deliver it in time?'

'Max smiled. 'Not only that Jack, I can turn your shitty little periodical into a mainstream best seller. I can give you a place in history. I can make you a force that will change the world!'

I snorted in derision. 'Like I said, I'm desperate so there's no need for the hyperbole, just say yes or no.'

'Then it's yes, but I'm not exaggerating. Here, let me show you something.'

Whines & spirits

He turned and led the way into an office which might have had a previous life as a broom cupboard and pointed to an ancient Remington typewriter.

'Good grief!' I exclaimed, 'if you write your stuff on that, no wonder you have trouble meeting your schedules. Have you never heard of the word processor or the PC?'

'It's not mine,' he replied, 'it belonged to a guy called Ivan Hammond, the greatest investigator of the occult that the world has ever seen. I got to know him through my own research and learned that he had uncovered a secret he believed to be so great that the fate of the world could be determined by its revelation or its concealment. And he offered to share it with me, both to divide the burden of that dreadful truth and because he feared for his life. You see, he felt that some force might seek to protect the secret.

'When I last saw him, he was working at this very machine, with a pile of completed pages stacked at one side. "Come back in an hour," he said, "and I will give you a story that will shake your world and maybe make you famous too." When I returned, he was dead, sitting before his typewriter, just as I had left him.'

'Dead?' I whispered.

'Yeah, well he was ninety-three, so who knows,' smiled Max, thinly.

'And what of his writing?'

'Every page was blank.'

'Blank?'

Empty promises

'That's right; something, some force, some entity, had ensured the secret was kept.'

'So, what's the story you're offering me?' I asked, looking round and spying a laptop and printer on a table inside the open bedroom door.

'The same one as Ivan; what I've told you happened twenty years ago. The only clue I had then to his researches was the name of a book he had casually mentioned during our discussions. And so, I set out on the trail he had pioneered, following the same leads, searching through the same arcane records, deciphering the same ancient parchments, until at last I've come within reach of that same goal.'

'Write it up and I'll collect it at noon on Thursday,' I said, cutting through Max's florid narrative.

'Can we discuss the matter of an advance?' he asked, as I turned to leave and, given that he had me over a barrel, I reached reluctantly into my jacket and removed my chequebook.

We spent the next day in frantic preparation: sourcing the photographs that Max had suggested might support his editorial and re-jigging the entire layout to accommodate his anticipated ten thousand words.

Late on Friday morning I left Mike tidying up around the edges and, crossing to Max's building, climbed the narrow flight of stairs to his landing. There was no answer to my knock and I pushed the door open and stepped inside.

Whines & spirits

Across the grubby kitchen I could see the open bedroom door and Max's laptop. Beside it, in the printer's out-tray, a neat pile of A4. I stepped tentatively across the worn vinyl and peered into the bedroom.

I was already reaching for the stack of paper when I caught sight of the figure that lay sprawled across the bed, the off-white duvet entwined around one leg, an arm hanging untidily down, knuckles brushing the floor.

As I took an involuntary inward breath, Max groaned, stretched and half lifted his head.

'Oh, hi Jack. Wassa time?' he enquired blearily and then his eyes snapped fully open and he pushed himself into a sitting position and regarded me uncertainly.

'You come for the article?' he asked, rather unnecessarily, since I was already leafing through the pages.

I looked across at him sharply and saw some sort of understanding flicker across his features. 'Yes,' I said, in answer to his question, 'but every one of these pages is blank.'

I had to hand it to him. He looked bemused, then shocked, and finally awed before letting out a slow, exhalation, his eyes widening in disbelief.

'But, Jack, that's just, just...spooky.'

You know, life's not so bad at Macramé Monthly; the pressure to shock and intrigue has been replaced by a monthly quest for colourful

Empty promises

potholders and napkin rings and in some ways I'm grateful to Max for his final failure. I still have no idea whether those pages were blank as a result of his lethargy or through occult intervention but I do know this, I won't be calling on him for our next article on hand-knotted water-bottle covers.

Hereafter

Pastor Brandon W O'Dacey had died quietly during the night, and now he was standing, a trifle impatiently, in what he assumed to be an anteroom to paradise.

He examined his surroundings with no little irritation: walls of a misty, luminescence; floor obscured by shifting skeins of mist and, overhead, a China blue sky revealed and concealed by drifting white clouds. It was all a mite theatrical, no doubt intended to offer reassurance to those of a nervous disposition, but hardly necessary for someone with his credentials.

He had, after all, devoted the last sixty years of his existence to promoting the afterlife and might, consequently, have expected to receive some sort of welcome on his eventual arrival at its portal. He suspected the usual procedural foul-up. He'd passed-over a shade after midnight and some bureaucratic son-of-a-bitch working to the twenty-four-hour clock was probably expecting him at noon. Goddam incompetents! He'd been surrounded by people like that for years, small brains and even smaller ambitions.

But *he'd* thought big, right from the start. Folks needed guidance and he'd given it, in spades. Heck, there'd been eight thousand at the '85 rally! Eight thousand poor souls crying out for comfort - and

Hereafter

that was just the beginning. With TV and the Internet, he'd topped three and a quarter million followers by ninety-two and after that the only way was up.

Of course, you couldn't run an outfit like that on faith alone. It took money too - a whole heap of money. But they'd been willing - his flock, and they'd understood how, if he seemed to be living high on the hog, it was only so's he could spread the good word and bring even more of sufferin' humanity into the church – his church. And they came: the sick, the destitute, the inebriated. Ev'ry no 'count, ornery deadbeat – hoping for deliverance from drudgery, pain and poverty and yet able to contribute nothing to assist in his mission. Still he had tolerated them, camping outside the gates of his estate, befouling God's good Earth. Until, he remembered, the bums had surged onto the road one day and, as he raised the limo's window to seal himself away, his eyes had caught and, for a moment held, those of his own father, vacant and lost to drink. Later, he'd watched from his rooftop balcony as the police cleared the area and he'd offered them a blessing from his distant vantage point.

His mother had died when he was born and, after her husband began a descent into alcoholism, an old aunt had raised him, using the cane and a sharp tongue to gain his compliance. It was through her that he came to understand that only the strong had merit and that the inadequate were to be despised. And, in between, he had realised, were the mass of humanity who were neither resolute nor despairing but who awaited God's guidance and direction.

It was their needs that had amassed him fame and fortune and a life of comfort, which was no more than was right, given his crusade for all that was decent in a wicked world.

Now he stood and waited and, after what might have been a heartbeat, had he any longer possessed a heart, he became slowly aware of a presence, tall, gowned and with folded wings, silhouetted against the pale light.

'Hallelujah!' he exclaimed, taking a tentative step towards the figure, 'you are, I assume, the angel who has come to escort me into the precincts of heaven? You have no idea how long and hard has been my journey thus far. It is, I truly believe, time for my reward!'

'Oh, I agree,' replied the entity, unfurling its wide wings which, Brandon W O'Dacey saw to his concern, were not feathery white but were dark, translucent skin, stretched between long fingers of bone.

The bottom of the garden

'Jennie, Jennie, what is all this, love?' Ted waved his hand distractedly at the strange assemblage of cakes and savouries spread across the flower border. Things had not been right for a while, he knew that; there had been signs, small eccentricities in his sister's behaviour. An obsession with folding and refolding towels and teacloths; a habit of concealing items from the morning mail. Nothing he'd not been able to dismiss as trivial, and yet – actions which led to inevitable concerns, reluctant diagnoses of approaching dementia.

And now this, something else again, food strewn through the roses, the contents of the pantry cast across the brown, autumn soil.

He stared in confusion, as she stood, arms hugging protectively her own gaunt frame. He couldn't read her expression; was it, expectation? Satisfaction? He walked across to her and grasped her shoulders in his big, veined hands and stared intently into her eyes.

'Jennie, what's this all about? Do you know why you've done this?'

For a moment she refused to engage with him, angled her face away, turned her eyes towards the

The bottom of the garden

ground. Then suddenly, she pulled back and swung her head to meet his gaze.

'Well of course I know, Edward,' she said, almost in a whisper. 'It's only you who do not understand.'

'Me?' He frowned. That was right enough he conceded; he didn't understand. 'Then tell me,' he urged, 'what do I need to know?'

'They are so hungry Edward. So hungry.'

'Who?' He could feel his frustration turning slowly to anger. 'Who's bloody hungry? The birds? You've got a cupboard full of sunflower seed to feed the birds, Jennie. They don't need this stuff – besides, it's probably not good for them; too much sugar, additives, 'E' numbers, that kind of thing. And don't you realise how much these things cost? You can't afford to throw them out for the wildlife...' he paused, a new line of persuasion suggesting itself, '...like rats, Jennie. You don't want rats in the garden, do you?'

'They won't let the rats come.' She shook her head emphatically.

'Who won't?'

'The fairies, Edward, they won't let anything hurt me.'

He stared, aghast. Whatever his suspicions concerning her mental health, he had never, for one moment, considered that things might be as bad as this, her deterioration so advanced.

'Fairies?' He had no idea how to deal with the situation. 'Fairies? There...there are no such things as fairies, Jennie! You know that,' he added, hopelessly.

'Oh, but there are, they come every night and speak to me. And I feed them because they are hungry, Edward.'

Oh Jennie...' he trailed off not knowing what to say next. The best thing was to get her inside. Get her sleeping pills down her and make her comfortable for the night. Tomorrow he'd call her doctor. Ask him to run tests, or whatever they did to check for Alzheimer's. Write to Social Services, was that how it worked? He sighed. His sister was ten years his senior and *he* was pushing seventy. In the end, time caught up with you; nobody went on forever. Their mother had been fond of saying that but he'd never found it particularly comforting. He looked down at the dirt-smeared icing and grubby pastry. Maybe this is what was waiting for him, a few years up the line. He put his arm gently round his sister's neck and led her back to the house.

'It's the vermin you see, I hear them foraging around down there, in the dark. Otherwise, I wouldn't mention it.'

Ted looked off to where the garden sloped away down to the copse. It was probably home to all kinds of wild creatures: foxes, badgers, those damn rats; he turned back to the woman confronting him from the far side of the hedge.

'She not well,' he began awkwardly, 'my sister; she doesn't always realise what she's doing. I'll clear it up later; when we get back from the hospital.'

The bottom of the garden

And this would be the third time he'd grovel around on his hands and knees, filling a plastic carrier with spoiled food. Heaven knew how many other occasions there had been when the wildlife had beaten him to it. The neighbour was right - even if the old bag *was* making a meal of it.

'And I'm worried about my cat, she's attracted by the smell. If you see her down there, shoo her back home. I hate to think what she might catch.'

He nodded briefly, suppressing his annoyance with the woman's lack of sympathy. 'I'll keep an eye out,' he said, and headed back for the house.

Ted sat back in disgust and then, pulling a supporting cane from one of the roses, prodded tentatively at the tattered remains. There were fur and bones but not much in the way of attached flesh. He tossed the bag of crumbling sponge cake and sausage rolls onto the lawn behind him and contemplated his discovery thoughtfully. From the colour, this was almost certainly all that was left of the old dear's ginger moggy. God knows how he was going to tell her it had been devoured by...he supposed it had to be a fox. There weren't any other carnivores loose in the English countryside that were capable of dismembering a cat so completely – were there? He'd read the odd story about puma and such like, loose in the Home Counties but...Mother of Mary, surely Jennie's cupcakes hadn't attracted a mountain lion into 34 Sycamore

Avenue? It sounded preposterous – until you considered the remains, that is.

Whatever he did next, the neighbour was going to hold his sister responsible so the least inflammatory option was to have the cat simply disappear. He climbed uncomfortably to his feet and set off to find a spade.

He'd seen her, the previous afternoon, when he'd come round to liaise with Jennie's new carer, peering into the foliage adjacent to the rose bed and calling its name. He'd felt guilty then; knowing that the cat was buried just a few yards from where she was searching but it was too late to acquaint her with its death and admit his own complicity in the cover up.

Today, her garden was deserted, the woman having apparently given up the hunt for her pet and Ted judged it safe to break cover and check the borders for more of his sister's largess. It was too soon, the doctor had explained, for the medication to have brought Jennie's erratic behaviour under control, and Ted suspected that she still felt a compulsion to provide sustenance for the garden's imaginary inhabitants.

He rummaged in a drawer, extracted a bag and, having checked that his sister was still sleeping off her lunch, quietly exited by the kitchen door.

He made his way down the path, glancing cautiously across to the neighbouring property but there were no signs of movement there. He stopped

The bottom of the garden

at the shed and collected a lawn rake, the best tool, he had found, with which to retrieve debris from amongst the roses' thorny, arching stems. Then he walked on to where the leaves of the trees at the edge of the copse danced against the summer sun.

He squatted down and squinted into the shadows amongst the roots. Yes, damn it! She'd been at it again; he could see a slice of some strawberry coloured confection there, near the back. He pushed the rake between the tangle of stems, and then, with some difficulty, dragged it back to the lawn's edge. He readied his bag, reached down to retrieve the item and gagged.

Bile rose in his gut, blood thumped at his temples; he staggered back collapsing onto the turf, hands thrust out desperately to steady his descent.

It wasn't a bakery delight wedged between the tines; it was a small, pink slipper enclosing a human foot, neatly severed at the ankle.

'You haven't been into the garden for a long time, Jennie.' Ted stood in the big bay window surveying the view. He could think of several reasons for avoiding the pastoral delights to the rear of Sycamore Avenue but his sister had been spared the horror of her neighbour's demise and he was careful not to arouse her concern even by omission.

The inquest had concluded that the old lady had died from heart failure brought on by strain and anxiety over her lost cat, and that, overnight, as her

Whines & spirits

body lay hidden by deep undergrowth, it had been subjected to depredation by scavenging foxes.

The local paper had made much of the tale and the subsequent public campaign, spurred on by concern for the safety of children and a largely unfounded fear of rabies, had resulted in a cull of all the animals resident in the copse.

Jennie knew nothing of this. Social Services had agreed that it was best she was not present during the forensic investigations and had arranged for her to spend a few days in respite care.

Ted looked round to the big armchair where his sister spent so much of her time. 'Eh, Jennie?' he persisted, anxious to determine whether she had recovered from her delusional state.

'No Edward,' she looked up at him, with a smile of resignation, 'there's no reason to go into the garden anymore.'

He smiled back. Things had reached some kind of stasis. She would never fully recover her mental acuity but, with luck, they could keep her free from fantasy.

'I think *I'll* just go for a stroll down to the copse,' he said, deciding on a whim to exorcise the demons of recent events, 'before it gets completely dark. I'll put the kettle on and when I come back, I'll make us a nice cuppa; how's that?

The garden was mostly in shadow, although the vanished sun still lit the cold, blue vacancy of the western sky, turning the woodland into a fretted, cut-paper, silhouette. It reminded Ted of a children's book which he and Jennie had shared as

The bottom of the garden

a Christmas present a long, long time ago. He stood quietly, hands thrust into his trousers' pockets against the chill, as the light faded and the hard, bright stars slowly appeared.

The copse would be empty now: scoured of life. He could understand the need for a response to events but he doubted that the clearance had achieved much, merely driven the surviving denizens to a new location; and something about that thought troubled him especially. *No reason to go into the garden any more.* No reason - to go into - *the garden.* Fear traced its way fleetingly along his spine and he turned quickly and ran back across the black-bladed lawn.

He heard the noises before he reached the house: the scrabbling and chittering; the sharp, urgent breathing; the rasp and snap. For a second, he paused, his hand enfolding the handle and then he wrenched the door open and stepped inside.

Turn for the worse

It was a bone-freezing winter's night with the ice-silver moon chased and buried by a great bank of blue-black cloud and the cold brush of fingers across your face was the first drift of snow down from the high arctic.

The only sensible place to be was the warm and welcoming haven of the Barley Mow and a table drawn up near to the blazing inglenook.

We exchanged greetings, unwound scarves, stamped feet, extended hands towards the flames and carried the first round of over-brimming glasses from the bar.

To begin with, the talk was of nothing consequential: the weather, the big match, the latest movie. It wasn't until the second tray of drinks had been purchased and sampled and an introspective silence had descended on the group that Maggie suggested it was a night for the telling of tales.

'You know,' she urged, 'something to send a shiver down your spine. Make you scared to walk home in the dark, alone!'

'A ghost story,' said Ben, as if the suggestion needed clarification.

His girlfriend, Jane, snorted derisorily and rolled her eyes towards the inn's low, beamed ceiling but

Turn for the worse

Toby, who had been staring into the fire for several minutes turned and fixed us with a steady gaze.

'I can tell you a story like that,' he said, 'if you want to hear it,' and, taking our silence for affirmation, he continued, 'it was just last year on All Hallow's Eve, on a lonely road over the Downs, not so far from here.

'The owner of Pagefoot Manor, Sir Irvin McDowd was driving across that open, bare-backed hillside above the old chalk pit at Upper Stoke. I called it a road although, in truth, it isn't much more than a farm track, but it provided a short cut back to the Manor and avoided a good five miles of motoring by the conventional route.

It was a foul night with rain driving in on a hard, south-easter from the Channel and visibility was so poor that the car's headlights only revealed the figure stumbling along the rutted lane at the very last moment. The walker was wrapped in a long coat with a hood pulled down against the weather and the rain was streaming from every fold of the material as he, or she, turned and waited for the car to draw alongside.

'"Get in," ordered the driver, "you'll drown in this downpour," and the figure nodded and climbed into the rear of the vehicle.

'Sir Irvin put the car into gear and pulled away into the storm but when he asked his passenger where he was headed, he got no more than a grunt in reply and soon the stranger seemed to fall asleep, the face still hidden by the hood...'

'For God's sake, Toby!' It was Jane again, pulling

Whines & spirits

another scornful face. 'We've all heard this one a thousand times. It's one of those "urban myths". Where did you get it from - the Internet? I'll bet that the next day Sir Irv mentions the mysterious hitchhiker to his gardener and *he* says, "Gawd, that was old Fred who died in a storm twenty years ago!" Am I right?'

'No,' replied Toby, unruffled by the interruption, 'not quite. The next thing that happened was that I woke up in an old cattle-shed, still wet through and with the hood of my coat plastered to my head.'

'You?!' I exclaimed. 'The walker was you? So, there wasn't a ghost after all! You had us going there for a bit. And I must say, that given how you ignored your rescuer and fell asleep in his car, I'm not surprised that Old Sir Irvin McWhatnot dumped you in that shed before he finished his journey home.'

'No ghost, you say?' The voice was that of the landlord, who had paused at our table whilst collecting empty glasses and had been following Toby's narration with interest. 'Well now, that depends on your point of view, I reckon.'

'How do you mean?' asked Mike.

'I mean that I used to see Sir Irvin driving that route over the Downs pretty regularly even though I know Lady Muriel begged him not to.

'Why, was it dangerous?'

'I reckon you'd say so, given that one night, with a storm blowing in from the south east, he missed a turn and drove over the edge of the chalk pit. The car was nothing but mangled wreckage by the time

Turn for the worse

it came to rest and the same, I suppose, could be said for poor old Sir Irvin. Of course, I don't recall that much about it because I was only a boy at the time.'

'A boy?' I repeated, tremulously.'

The landlord gathered up the last glass and turned for the bar. "Yeah, well he died thirty years ago come October 31st, didn't he?'

I gave Maggie a lift when we left; she wouldn't walk home alone.

Our kind

We learned everything, little by little, year by year, because in that way, Cousin Iorghu said, the day would come when we would know all that we needed to know about the world. Even then, I thought I could see a difference between need and desire but I was too young to untangle the thought and tease it out into a question for Grandfather Stravechi.

By the time I was seven I understood that the forest at night was a dangerous place and that the paths that wound among the tall, dark trunks and slipped through the fern-shrouded gullies, were places to approach with caution, especially when the moon was full; and yet, when I stood high, on the big rock, where the fir trees thinned and fingers of loose scree from the mountain sifted down towards the old lodge, I looked far into the distant valley and my mind was filled with excited anticipation.

Iorghu had told us all the ancient tales concerning the night prowler's search for blood; the midnight encounters, the inhuman cruelty. Grandfather Stravechi's own brother Marek had died that way and our patriarch still remembered the cacophony of voices, and the flaring torch light as the villagers

Our kind

rose up and took retribution against their ancient foe.

'We must always stand together,' said Iorghu, 'against the evil among us. We are an ancient people who will not be driven from our home.'

We were teenagers by then, Jacek and I, with that angry urge for justice that inspires the young and an even greater need of adventure. Our family's lives, we reasoned, had been in jeopardy long enough. We would hunt out the wickedness that lived among us, whatever the cost. And so, one night we slipped from the house and set off towards the pass, where we knew one of their kind had his home.

The sky was filled with dark, ragged cloud as we plunged quickly down through the bracken and into the shadowy wood that fringed our quarry's property. With infinite care we crawled up towards the single, uncurtained window and peered in.

A young girl sat at an oak table lit by a candle in a stout, wooden holder. She was bending towards a frame of needlework and the action exposed the pale, ivory skin of her neck.

In that instant I was consumed with desire. I drew my cloak around me and stepped up onto the window's ledge and at that moment as the moon broke clear of the overcast and bathed us in its full glory, I looked across at Jacek and he grinned back, his long white incisors drawing a wet trickle of blood from his thin, white lips.

Against the grain

'There's something odd about that tree.' Mrs Rawlings adjusted her glasses and squinted myopically through the cottage's latticed windows at the imposing form of the oak on the edge of the front lawn.

'What's that, the tree? Oh yes, very...sculptural,' replied Daniel distractedly as he reached through the mop and broom heads in an attempt to replace the screw which secured the fuse-box cover.

'The shape,' continued his mother, 'that's what it is, the shape.'

'Shape?' said Daniel, swearing quietly as the screw slipped from his fingers and vanished somewhere behind the vacuum.

'Yes, the shape, it's changed – and don't swear Daniel, your father used to say that it displays a want of vocabulary.'

'Sorry, didn't think you were listening.'

'Well I was, whereas you haven't heard a word I've said for the last five minutes.'

'Yes I have,' insisted her son, lifting the cupboard's contents, item by item, onto the kitchen's stone floor, 'you were talking about the tree.'

'Yes, and what about the tree?'

'S'very...attractive.'

'You see? I said no such thing; I'm trying to tell you

that it has altered its shape – since I moved in on Monday.'

'Its shape?' Daniel rose uncomfortably from where he squatted among the cleaning utensils and studied the tree with exaggerated intensity. 'What's wrong with its shape? It looks like a fine example of an English oak to me.'

'There's nothing wrong, it's just different – since I stood here yesterday admiring the view across to the Downs.'

'Well, it'll be the wind,' said Daniel, 'blown the branches about a bit since then, rearranged the leaves.'

'Daniel, I know you doubt my ability to live her on my own given my advanced stage of decrepitude but senility is not one of my disabilities. On Tuesday, after lunch, I was washing up at this sink and considering how fortunate I was to have purchased this beautiful cottage, in this wonderful location and noting how one of the contributing features was the distant view of the windmill on Old Sopton Down.'

Mrs Rawlings paused, assured herself of her son's full attention and continued, 'today, there is no such view. It is obscured by one of the oak's branches. See for yourself.'

Daniel sighed, placed the screwdriver on the drainer and dutifully applied himself to appraising the scenic wonders of Milden Stracey as seen from the AGA enhanced, flagstone-floored, diamond-paned delights of Filbert Cottage.

Whines & spirits

'There is no view of the windmill on Old Sopton Down,' he announced after a reasonable amount of time for proper scrutiny had elapsed. 'The tree is in the way...'

Mrs Rawlings folded her arms and adopted an expression intended to convey her belated satisfaction with this conclusion.

'...and if there's no view of the windmill today, then there was no view of it yesterday.'

Mrs Rawlings frowned. 'From this very spot,' she said with just enough emphasis to show that a denial was unwelcome.

'But Mum, there can't have been. That's a blood...a very big branch and you can be sure it hasn't moved anywhere for... I don't know, twenty years?'

'Have you finished fixing that fuse,' said Mrs Rawlings, 'because, if you have, it's time you were getting back home for your dinner, don't you think?'

'What's the matter with the tree, dear?' Millicent Heathcote-Smith carefully replaced her bone-china cup in its saucer and looked up into the branches angling above her. 'I must say, I think it's magnificent. Like being in a great, green tent.' Above her the oak's canopy swayed and rustled in the breeze.

'I'm not sure,' said her friend, following her gaze into the high interior of the foliage, 'It's just a feeling really. There's just...' her voice dropped away and

Against the grain

she raised her own cup and took a long sip of Earl Grey.

'Just what, dear?'

'Oh Millie, that's why I asked you over. You know about these things.'

'What things?'

'Don't be so disingenuous Millie, you know what I mean: astrology, palm reading, spiritualism. Unnatural phenomenon...' Gladys Rawlings regarded her friend for a moment and, finding her receptive, plunged on, 'I've been here six months now and I love everything about the cottage, except...'

'This tree.'

'This tree. I sweep the leaves into a tidy pile and when I return with a bin I find them distributed evenly all around the lawn although there's no wind blowing. I attempt to saw off some untidy growth around the trunk and I'm overcome with a feeling of nausea and have to lie down for an hour. When I park on the gravel beneath it, I find the car coated with sap or resin or something – Daniel says it's the greenfly, and maybe he's right but, Millie, I don't feel comfortable sitting here right now; I have this overwhelming feeling that I'm not welcome. I know it's silly... and I'm sorry, I wish I'd never mentioned it. Do you think I'm suffering from depression or paranoia?'

'Paranoia? Don't be ridiculous Gladys. I certainly think you're in a highly susceptible state of mind. Your husband died just last year, you've uprooted yourself from the family home and relocated into

Whines & spirits

the depths of the country; your whole being is in a state of excited agitation – it makes you a target for unfamiliar forces.'

'Unfamiliar forces? Whatever do you mean Millie? Poltergeist? I thought they only affected young people not octogenarians.'

'No, not a poltergeist, dear – a dryad, a spirit of the tree.'

'I know what dryads are Millie, I majored in Classics a very long time ago. But I don't recall anything about them being vindictive or spiteful so why am I getting the treatment?'

'Maybe she's just trying to warn you off. You're new to the cottage and your intentions aren't clear. I've no doubt that if you show you have no evil intentions, everything will soon settle down.'

'Millie, this is madness! It's the twenty-first century for heaven's sake. Am I expected to believe in faeries at my age? No, don't protest, I asked for your interpretation of events and I'm keeping an open mind. I'll make sure to treat the oak with all due deference and if that doesn't work there's always the ultimate deterrent.'

Millicent's hand paused, en route to the chocolate digestives, and she raised a quizzical eyebrow.

'You've cut the bloody tree down!' Daniel Rawlings stood beside his car and stared incredulously at the neat stump and scattering of sawdust.

'Language Daniel! And I had no choice, after what happened; come inside dear and I'll tell you all

Against the grain

about it over a slice of your favourite fruit cake.'

In fact, Gladys Rawlings had no intention of telling her son of the events which had led up to the felling of the oak. She was perfectly sure that if she described how she had been woken during the night by leaves scraping across her window he would point out, quite correctly, that the oak stood thirty feet from her bedroom and that even the longest bough was incapable of reaching so far. And yet, night after night she had lay in the dark and listened to their rasping against the glass and watched their smudgy shadows, cast by the moon, fluttering down the wall towards her bed.

'I never did get the hang of that automatic you insisted I should buy after my arthritis set in. I must have stepped on the accelerator instead of the brake I suppose. Anyway, Gary said the tree wasn't safe afterwards and it would have to come down.'

'Afterwards, what do you mean "afterwards" – and who's Gary?'

'After I hit it, dear – the tree – and Gary is a charming young man from the village. He's quite an entrepreneur in his way - gardener, tree surgeon, builder - as he says, you have to turn your hand to anything these days to make a living.' Mrs Rawlings became aware that she was talking too much. It wasn't that she was seeking to justify her actions – she had slept peacefully for the first time in weeks, since the tree had been removed – but she was feeling guilt over the lie she was telling to gain her son's acceptance. She paused to observe his reactions thus far.

Whines & spirits

'So you ran into the oak – are you sure you're OK? And then you found this cowboy, Gary, to take it down? Don't you need planning consent to fell a tree, Mum?'

'Yes, I'm perfectly all right and Gary isn't a cowboy. He says he'll confirm that the tree was unsafe if anyone asks any questions although, since I'm on a road to nowhere, it's unlikely that anyone will.'

'Hmmph. Good for Gary. Well I suppose it's too late to discuss it now – the tree's gone.'

It was only when Daniel was halfway back along the road to his own home that he thought to wonder about the damage to his mother's car.

'It's dry rot Mrs Rawlings,' Gary Salter stepped down from the stepladder from which he had been examining the ceiling timbers of Filbert Cottage's main bedroom and dusted his hands on the front of his overalls. 'But don't you worry, it's only one rail and it ain't load bearing, more decorative if you get my meaning. I can fix it no trouble. I've gotta nice bit a green oak down at the yard.'

She was a nice old biddy, Mrs Rawlings and a good customer too, Gary reflected, as he turned his van out of the cottage drive, even if she was a touch eccentric at times. Look at that effin' tree! Nice old oak, in Gary's opinion, but she'd been determined to have it down and who was he to argue? Sod the planners! He'd made three-hundred quid on that job, plus the value of the timber, and now he was

Against the grain

selling it back to her he'd make a bit more - which was perfectly OK - he'd had to cart it off and store it and get it cut up – so it was fair enough, although he'd rather she didn't put two and two together and make five.

Mrs Rawlings lay in her bed and stared at the pale shape of the new timber crossing the ceiling above her head. She had been woken from a deep sleep by the sound of leaves, brushing impossibly across her walls. Now, she lay immobile, and watched the shadows of a moonless night crowd in around her.

Starfighter

The old man pulled off his greasy cap and wiped a ragged, crimson cuff across his brow. The sack was small but heavy, the worn hessian stretched into small soft curves and hard protrusions. He had dragged it to the top of the caravan's three decaying steps and now he stood in the doorway, regaining his breath and looking out onto the empty October field. The meadow grass was dark and wet and beside the bramble-tangled hedge a lean, piebald mare pulled at the tussocks and snorted smoky breath into the expectant, autumn air. With a final effort the man pushed back into the trailer's dark interior and the paint-flaked door swung shut behind him.

The caravan stood silently in the field's corner, fading as the year was fading; nightshade lacing the spoked wheels, colours peeling in drab moss greens, fungal yellows, and reds like long-dried blood; warped, split, spider-creviced, with the thick, clammy, coffin-rotted smell of decay.

Danny flew down the golden-leaved lane heading for home in his imaginary starfighter; arms stretched to feel the wind; a banking turn towards

Starfighter

the distant church spire; a course correction past the fallen oak. He was tea-time late and heading for trouble but there had been trees to climb and camps to build and when he had waved a last salute to his friends and peeled away for the descent to the village, the six o'clock bell had been announcing his court martial. So he opened the thrusters and fired the after-burners and his feet skidded on the loose flints and slipped on the slick-green chalk and as he rounded the turn by the old farm he lost control and tumbled into the gateless field and lay winded, among the trailing skeins of early-evening mist, snaking in from the river.

When he climbed to his knees and looked around, his eyes widened and his mouth opened in a silent 'Oh!' How could he not have known about the fair? He'd seen no bills pasted, heard no excited stories, received no parental warnings and yet, here in the church-field were a riot of stalls and stands, tents and rides. Over there, a hoopla, a switchback, a helter-skelter; a tall red and yellow "test your strength" surmounted by a bright, brass bell; a row of white posts and red cups and a massive pile of coconuts; the vacant swinging chairs of a big wheel – vacant because, he suddenly realised, the fairground was deserted, unlit. Only one attraction was illuminated: on the far side of the field, at the end of an avenue of shadowed shooting ranges and tombolas, carousels and dartboards, stood a caravan, bedecked in lights, sparkling in crisp reds and vibrant greens, it's sharp, carved mouldings shining gold.

Whines & spirits

Danny climbed to his feet and walked hesitantly towards it. He could see now that the caravan stood beside a huge and extravagantly decorated canvas on which was depicted a view of the cosmos; where silver satellite moons circled glowing gas giants and mysterious purple nebulae twisted among dusty, diamond star-fields, all spiralling down into the blank, empty mouth of a vast black hole, which was indeed, a round, black hole in the painted scene and into which ran a pair of iron rails. Sitting astride the rails was a flame-painted spaceship: chrome trimmed, red-padded, stubby-winged. Danny reached it and ran his fingers over the sparkling, crystal surface.

'Well, are you going to take a ride, boy?' It was a man stepping down jauntily from the caravan's dazzling, glass-reflected, lamp-lit interior. He wore a splendid crimson jacket with gold braid and a matching cap and his eyes were a colour that Danny had never realised eyes could be.

'Where does it go?' Danny asked, returning his gaze to the wonderful cosmic rail car.

'Where would you like it to go?' The man had walked across and behind the row of railings, which separated the ride from the fairground and he had his hand on the gate that gave entrance to the track.

'Mars!' cried Danny without a moment's hesitation, 'but,' he added suddenly disconsolate, 'I've no money to pay you with.'

'Ah well, you see the fair's not open and so there's no charge,' replied the man with a bone-white smile and he threw the gate wide and Danny stepped eagerly inside and up into the gleaming craft. At the throw of a handle the railcar spun slowly on its axis and in that instant Danny had time to see the name of the black-hole ride, written in curling silver letters above the painted universe.

'Soulstealer,' mouthed Danny, just before the car plunged forward into the sightless void.

The string-tied sack was small but heavy, the worn hessian stretched into small soft curves and hard protrusions. At the top of the caravan's three rotting steps the old man stood, regaining his breath and looking out onto the empty October field. As the Hallowe'en moon rose above the churchyard, what might have been the shadow of a small boy flickered briefly across the grass.

The rat

They laid the prince within the castle's vaults. There, attracted by his already decomposing corpse, the rat climbed into the open coffin and found itself trapped as the lid was sealed.

Visiting her dead lover's tomb, the girl, hearing scrabbling from within, tore frantic hands on the rough stone and wrenched the lid from the sepulchre. The rat, driven mad by its incarceration, leapt free, burying its teeth into her pale neck. As she died, she placed one final kiss and smeared the prince's mouth with gore.

Thus misdirected, they drove an oak stake through his heart, to ensure conclusion.

Ring in the new

'So, you're a writer then?' I asked, perusing my customer with interest, as I carefully decanted an ice-cold beer from can to glass.

'That's right,' replied the man on the other side of the bar, his accent betraying his American origins, 'I'm on a field trip researching my next book, 'Whines and Spirits – that's "whine" as in...'

'Banshees and werewolves,' I interjected, 'yes, I get the idea,' and, noting he looked a trifle abashed at my prescience, I added, 'we get a lot of people visiting the area because of its history of matters...supernatural.'

'You certainly have a reputation,' agreed the other, taking a long, indulgent pull at his drink and then wiping the back of his hand theatrically across his lips. 'Yes sir! I expect to devote several chapters to your village and its various manifestations; the affair up at the vicarage; the goings on in Dogberry Lane; and, in particular, the strange tale of the Brockdale bells. I believe this very inn was involved in that latter tale, am I right?'

'Hardly involved,' I told him. 'Robbie Tredare set out from here alright, and so I suppose my predecessor at The Green Man was one of the last people to see him alive, but involved is putting it a bit strong.'

Ring in the new

'Even so, you'd know the story well,' insisted the writer, leaning forward eagerly, 'would that be so?'

'Well, I've certainly had reason to tell it often enough,' I replied wearily, 'Old Sam Pekinsport left a full account in his diary and he left that in the pub,' and I gestured towards the display case lodged between the whisky and gin optics.

'And he would have been the landlord, back in 1799 when Tredare set off?'

'That's right. As you'll know, it was the very last day of that year and Robbie was planning to ring the Brockdale bells to see in the new century. He left here around ten; it's over four miles to Saint Agnes and its rough moorland all the way.'

'Was there no bell ringer in Brockdale?'

'Ah! There were no people in Brockdale! No more are there today. It's been deserted since 1665 when plague took the whole population: squire and ploughboy. After that the place fell into ruin, all except for the church, which continued to be tended for several decades by people who lived around the moor. Eventually though, even their interest waned, until only the marking of the year's passage by the bells remained. By 1799 it was more by custom than dedication, tradition rather than religious commitment. And the building was in serious disrepair; the windows blown in, no tiles on the roof of the nave, cracks in the masonry. I doubt whether anyone would have continued the practice if Robbie Tredare had retired – as it was the question never arose. He walked out of this bar on December 31 that year and never returned.'

Whines & spirits

'Vanished!' breathed the American, 'into thin air!'

'No such thing,' I retorted. 'I said he never returned, but he was found sure enough – under the ruins of the tower. It collapsed on him when he pulled on the bell rope. He was buried up on the moor and the church was left in ruins. No one would go near the place afterwards and they said that Robbie's ghost still sounded the bells every New Year's Eve, gathering souls to join the dead in the abandoned churchyard.'

'Wow! What a story! That's somewhere's I gotta visit! And its New Year on Friday so what say I retrace old Robbie's footsteps and see the year turn among the gravestones of Saint Agnes?'

'You're not afraid of the ghost?'

'Afraid? You think I believe that crap? Hey fella, I write this stuff for the gullible and the superstitious, of which there are, I am glad to say, enough to keep my bank balance more than healthy! A first-hand account of a night among the tombs will be worth a warehouse full of advance orders. I'll take my audio machine and record my experience as it happens, and if I meet up with Master Tredare, - don't be surprised!'

New Year at The Green Man was the usual hectic, noisy, joyful occasion and we went to bed late and slept soundly so that it was late on Saturday morning before I recalled the writer's intentions of the night before and crossed the yard to his room to hear of his adventure. But there was no reply to my knock and I put him out of my mind until the

Ring in the new

evening when he failed to appear for dinner. Then, with a mild sense of foreboding, I investigated further and found his suitcase and belongings still in his bedroom, his bed unused.

On Sunday I took an early breakfast, left Hilary and Matt to open up the pub, and with a beer and porkpie in my backpack I followed the route through the heather and over the hill to Brockdale.

It was a bright morning and mild, despite the season, and setting myself a brisk pace, I soon came within view of the ruins of Saint Agnes'. After two centuries it was little more than a pile of tumbled masonry, almost hidden among the gorse and granite of the moor and it took only a few minutes to satisfy myself that I was alone in the abandoned churchyard.

Unshouldering my pack, I looked around for somewhere to sit and enjoy my beer whilst I considered the mystery of my missing customer and an old, yet remarkably intact tomb, half buried by grass, caught my eye. As I approached it there was a glint of reflected light and reaching into the undergrowth, I withdrew a small, electronic recording device: it was the machine I had seen the American carrying that evening in The Green Man. If anything might reveal his fate I imagined, it was this, the writer's verbatim notes on his midnight sojourn beside the tumbled tower and, settling myself on the weathered stone slab I thumbed the playback button and held my breath.

For perhaps thirty seconds there was nothing but the soft, electronic hiss of white noise and then suddenly, clear and distinct, the impossible sound of Saint Agnes' bell, tolling out the old year and welcoming a new soul.

Future plans

Charlie bit into the sickly-sweet, insubstantial froth, grimaced and spat a pink, wet smear onto the muddy grass. Then he spat again, to clear his mouth of the chemical taste and tossed the candyfloss into a narrow, tarpaulin-walled alley between the sideshows.

The fair of his childhood memory was vast and fantastical: a cascade of lights and bevelled glass; piping organs and oil-painted tigers; bright colours and golden curlicues; barley-twist brass and barrel-topped caravans.

This event, on a wet, Wednesday afternoon behind the estate, was as degraded and artificial as the spun sugar, dissolving among the guy ropes.

Everything, from the overloud pop music to the amateurishly painted booths with their racks of grubby, felt toys, had conspired to annoy Charlie as he wandered aimlessly among the stalls.

It was all tat - not just the fair but life in general. People just didn't seem to have the motivation any more. He saw it day after day: rude shop assistants,

Future Plans

unhelpful council workers. Look at the guy at the Job Centre yesterday. What a clown! Did he really expect Charlie to apply for work stacking supermarket shelves? I've got a degree you know, Charlie had reminded him and the little git had had the temerity to suggest that there was satisfaction to be gained from any form of employment and did Charlie realise it had been two years now since he had signed on?

Ha! The tosser had walked right into that one! I know this office has been failing to find a position suited to my abilities for two years, Charlie had retorted with a sneer, and the guy hadn't had an answer to that one, had he? Couldn't defend his own inadequacies when he was confronted with them. Christ! Two bloody years Charlie had been tramping down there once every week and they couldn't pull their fingers out and find him proper work. What a bunch of ... . It was fortunate that Charlie didn't need the money; that his mother was around to do the shopping and cooking and deal with the bills. The money the state paid him in recompense for their failure to find him work wouldn't be nearly enough to cover stuff like that – hell, it barely met his petrol costs and a few drinks down at the Lion every night. It was a real struggle to save enough for the occasional holiday.

'Wanna know yer fortune, fella?' Charlie's train of thought was interrupted by a voice from an open-fronted tent adorned with silver-foil stars and moons. A sign above the entrance read, 'Rita – tarot cards and palm reading'.

Whines & spirits

Charlie peered inside. Rita, assuming it was she, was attractive, around seventeen, wore a pair of faded denim shorts and a Disney T shirt and, perhaps as a single concession to her trade, a pair of gold, hoop earrings. She was still far removed from Charlie's image of a shawl-draped crone with a crystal ball and her age and casual dress reinforced his impression of the fair's shoddy status.

'Y'er fortune,' repeated the girl, seeing Charlie's quizzical expression, 'only five quid – and I'm good, honest.'

'Oh yeah?' said Charlie, seeing at least the opportunity for some innocent amusement, 'learn it from a book, did you? Fortune Telling for Dummies?! No, I don't think so, luv, I've already wasted two pounds on a toxic candyfloss in your flea-bitten fair and I can manage without the "tall, dark stranger bit", ta.'

'S'yer funeral, Charlie,' replied the girl, with a shrug, crossing one long, bare leg over the other and closing her eyes.

'Hey, just a moment, how do you know my name?' Charlie regretted the question as soon as it left his lips. He hadn't meant to give credence to the girl's claims of clairvoyance; in fact, it was immediately obviously that she had simply heard someone speaking to him, and he remembered now, passing Mike on his way into the fair. They had called greetings to each other and Rita had clearly been within earshot. He opened his mouth to refute the implications of his question but Rita took the initiative.

Future Plans

'I know a lot more abhat you than that,' she said, raising her dark, shadowed lids and fixing him with a knowing gaze. 'Whatta you gotta lose, eh?' she grinned, charmingly, 'apart frum five quid that is! Sit dahn and I'll do yer palm fer half-price, ows that?'

Charlie had to smile; the kid was good; anyone less savvy than he was would be drawn in, hook, line and sinker. Well, she didn't know it yet but she'd met her match and it would be a valuable lesson in dealing with people who were her intellectual superiors.

'It's all bunkum,' he told her, placing his upturned palm into her small hand, 'but then, you already know that, don't you?'

'You ain't really ever grown up,' said Rita without preamble and apparently not in response to his derisive remark but as an introduction to her reading. She ran her own well-manicured index finger along a crease in his skin. 'Despite yer age, you ain't never taken responsibility fer yer life. Y'er twenty-six,' she added, confidently and Charlie's angry response was subdued by the accuracy of her information; she couldn't have got that statistic from his encounter with Mike.

'Y'er self-centred, too,' Rita continued, unabashed, 'you rely on uver people but you don't offer nuffin in return.'

'You've got a hell of a nerve! Who do I rely on? What other people?' Charlie scowled across the table at his accuser.

Whines & spirits

'Y'er muver fer one. You still live wiv y'er muver, don'ja?'

'What do you mean, "still",' blazed Charlie, snatching away his hand. 'What's that supposed to imply? And anyway, a lot you know, you little tart! My mother died of cancer, a year ago. I live alone. I don't need anyone holding my hand, either her - or you!' The lie came urgently to his lips. Why should he reveal how he conducted his life to this...this ignorant, gypsy kid; shooting in the dark and watching to see if her barbs drew blood? That was how they worked, wasn't it? Make a guess and see if it brought a response? He realised, with sudden chagrin, how well her plan had worked. He took a deep breath and brought himself under control.

'I thought you attempted to tell the future,' he said, evenly, 'not insult your clients with a skewed analysis of their motivations.'

'I don't know nuffin abaht yer future,' answered the girl, 'I said, did you wanna know yer fortune,' 'but I didn't say I'd tell it to you'.

'So you admit, it's a con?'

'You ain't paid yet,' Rita pointed out. 'But no, you ain't bein' 'ad. If you understand yerself properly, recognise 'ow ya fit inta the world, then you can work owt yer own future. But you need to accept the troof,' she added, pointedly.

'That is the truth,' growled Charlie, rising from his chair and throwing down a five-pound note. 'I live alone; I plough my own furrow; rely on no-one. I told you, my mother is dead, God rest her soul.'

Future Plans

'Amen,' whispered Rita, 'you go make yer own future,' and she watched as he strode from the tent and was lost in the swirling rain.

Charlie hurried on, his feet splashing through the muddied field, his collar raised against the growing storm. Out from the fair he ran, into the estate and along his garden path, wrenching open the door and scrubbing his feet on the mat.

His dripping coat consigned to the rack, he turned and stepped into the quiet kitchen. The usual signs of activity were absent. The hob empty of saucepans, the oven unlit.

He called into the hallway, 'Mum! I'm home,' and there was no reply. He climbed the stairs and crossed to his mother's room but the bed was stripped, the mattress bare and through the open wardrobe door he could see that the rails were empty.

Entombed

The figure wasn't in any way threatening despite the seven-foot spear clutched in his right hand and the cruel serrated dagger at his waist.

He'd clearly been dead for a very long time.

Behind desiccated lids the eye sockets were empty cavities, macabre miniatures of the dark cavern that the figure had been set to guard.

On his head a swath of cloth still showed, despite the ravages of time, a rich, purple stripe and a glint of gold. The material was knotted above one ear and fell in a long fold to the shoulders where its contours and colour were lost beneath the accumulated dust.

As the last of the sand from the roof-fall that had revealed the cave whispered down, Houghton raised his torch and examined the face more closely. The skin was almost black and deeply furrowed like the hard ridges of the palm trunks at the oasis where they had made camp earlier that month. It was a face shaped over centuries by slow mummification in the bone-dry desert air and yet...and yet, it seemed to Houghton that it was still not old enough.

The carved portal that the excavations had revealed and the massive stones of the entrance chamber beyond it, had indicated an origin in pre-history; the product of a community which had existed much earlier than any previously recorded in the valley. He had hoped that further finds might reveal the beginnings of the Cult of the Sorceress, the enigmatic religion that had guided the formation of a great empire in later centuries and which still held sway among the scattered tribes that represented all that remained of that once proud dominion.

The figures incised into the doorway behind him had raised his expectations with their references to the great goddess, but their warning of the tomb's perpetual guardian had dismayed and frightened the local men who formed the work-party and overnight he had found himself alone at the excavation.

It was an inconvenience more than a disaster; the heavy digging had been completed and clearing a route to the tomb was pretty much a one-man job. The loss of the field kitchen would be a problem eventually but for the moment he had sufficient supplies of canned food and bottled water and so he had decided to continue the work.

That morning he had cleared the stone doorway, which sealed the end of the corridor, and with the help of the Landrover's winch had hauled it aside only to discover a wall of sand barring further ingress. As he had prodded it disconsolately with his trowel it had given way leaving a space through which he had been able to crawl into the tomb, at which point the tunnel's structure had suddenly collapsed, with more sand pouring down from the ceiling above, filling the passageway, blocking his exit and disclosing the tomb's guardian.

Houghton had not panicked. He was confident that he could dig his way out through the loose sand and he had a powerful torch at his disposal; so he had turned his attention instead to the sentinel and that was when his doubts had surfaced.

Everything about the tomb – the carving, the set of the giant rocks, the sealed entrance, spoke to him of a vast antiquity, but the robed figure, though centuries old, could not be its contemporary. The dress style was that of a warrior from the Second Empire, a period divorced by seven millennia from the stone-age burial chamber and yet the man occupied a stone-cut niche apparently designed for his occupancy.

Houghton frowned and reached forward to take a fold of the dusty cloth between his finger and thumb.

The material had no substance; it dissolved into motes, which danced in the beam of his torch. He pulled his hand back in alarm at the destruction but the movement only served to disturb the air more and, as he watched, the figure crumbled remorselessly, the dust from its destruction forming a grey cloud around him. The purple turban turned to smoke, the hanging folds falling like thin, dry rain. Houghton cried out in despair and stepped up into the niche his fingers grasping at the grainy air in a futile attempt to save what was already lost. He found himself caught in a miasma of chocking particles, his eyes sticky, his nostrils clogged, his lungs drained. The last thing he saw clearly was the charred, parchment mask of the guardian's face as the sightless eyes merged with his own, then the torch fell from his grasp and smashed into darkness on the stony floor.

Entombed

As time passes the sand sifts down, its weight forcing the stone doorway closed and burying the entrance chamber and its portal.

Inside, the megalith's latest guardian stands silently, waiting for the world to end.

Countless times

There was something disconcerting about the ancient building and the manner in which it commanded the dark, tree-covered slopes. Its walls were sheer and windowless, breached only by a single, great gateway, which blocked the path up from the forest; the massive, timber doors secured with wide iron hinges and patterned by huge, hammered nail-heads. Set into one of the doors was a small postern.

'What d'you think Daisy, reckon they might put us up for the night?' asked my companion, reaching for the bell-pull.

I looked off into the crowded firs. As the moon cleared the distant peaks, something moved in the darkness among the ferns.

'What have we got to lose?' I wondered aloud.

'Transylvania!' I bent over the brochures spread across the table and looked aslant at Will, carelessly at ease in the pub's window seat, his long, sinewy limbs folded into the panelled recess. 'Are you serious?'

'Why not?' he replied. 'You said you wanted some real mountain cycling and the Carpathians are real mountains, take a look at the pictures.'

Countless times

'Yes, I can see that but I was thinking more, L'Alpe d'Huez or Col de la Madeleine.'

'Oh come on Daisy! Everyone wants to head to France and pretend they're on La Tour! The place'll be packed with road-race wannabees in their designer-label Lycra, prices will hit the roof and you won't see the view for motorised caravans. Romania, on the other hand, has hundreds of miles of deserted mountain roads and you can get a night's accommodation for the price of a Mars bar. It's a poor country,' he added, noting my raised eyebrows, 'the average wage is around £80 a week so we'll be helping the economy too!'

I smiled wanly. Will was an irresistible force and we both knew that however long we sparred, it would be his arguments that won the day.

'We'll want a roof over our heads, at night,' I replied, conceding his victory by implication,' there are some nasty things abroad in those forests after dark.'

'Ah, yes, vampires! Don't want to get bitten by the undead, do we Daisy?!'

I snorted, derisorily, both at his use of my usual epithet and at his childish attempt to provoke a nervous response.

The 'Daisy' came from 'Daisy Duke,' blonde nymphet of a defunct TV series. My surname being Duke, Will had thought it an appropriate reflection of what he perceived as my timidity.

'Wolves, Will,' I returned, without rancour, 'wolves and bears; they're both still wild in Romania; you have to watch your step.'

Whines & spirits

'Indeed you do,' he jumped to his feet and grinned at me engagingly. 'So, you're up for it then? I'll go ahead and make the booking,' and, despite all my reservations about our unresolved friendship, I nodded, in resignation.

We had cycling in common; had it not been for that I doubt that I would have chosen Will as a friend. He was brash and confident; I was introverted and lacking in self-esteem and I had little doubt it was those very weaknesses in my personality that led Will to cultivate my companionship. With me, he had no competition for his exuberance and no resistance to his intentions. I was, in short, his to command.

So it was that three months later we found ourselves cycling through the Western Carpathians; more specifically, the Apuseni Mountains, making our way from one medieval village to the next and spending each night in a different inn or one of the few local farmhouses that offered accommodation to foreign travellers. Because in that respect Will had proved to be correct: the region was far from the tourist circuit and, on the narrow roadways which swooped in and out of the tight, wooded valleys, the only traffic we encountered seemed to be from an earlier century.

On this particular day we had climbed our way high above the tree line and had expended time exploring the track ways and footpaths, which wound through the mountain pastures. In fact, we

Countless times

had spent so much time in this pursuit that when we at last consulted our map and took the steep downward path towards our next destination, it was already clear that we would not complete our journey before dark. And when the sun had disappeared behind the peaks and the valley plunged into shadow, we had begun to cast around for some sign of human habitation where we might hope to find food and shelter for the coming night.

It was then that we began to regret a little the remoteness of our chosen location and the paucity of fellow travellers, until Will spotted a light through the branches and we turned onto the wide, rutted driveway which led up to the castle's walls and the ironbound gate.

Will stood on his pedals, reached up for the ornate, weathered bell-pull and yanked on the handle, an action which yielded a shower of rusted metal and a ringing, far off yet clear in the silent mountain air.

'The place has probably been deserted for decades,' I suggested, regardless of the light that had first drawn his attention to the building. In truth, I wasn't anxious to disturb whoever lived beyond those formidable walls – not, I assured myself, because of any childish fears of what lurked in dark places - but simply because it seemed inappropriate and embarrassing to beg lodging from the local gentry.

If not a castle, then certainly a fortified manor or whatever might be the Romanian equivalent hereabouts and therefore the home of someone with money and independence who was likely to

Whines & spirits

disdain requests from sweaty, English push-bikers looking for B&B.

Will laughed at my concerned face, 'Don't worry Daisy, Vlad the Impaler died years ago - although,' he added, gurning at me over his shoulder as the handle on the postern gate began to turn, gratingly, 'that's not to say that he doesn't rise from his coffin as soon as the moon's up!'

I pulled a face to show my indifference to his humour and turned my attention to the figure that stood in the now open doorway.

He was short, stooped and wearing a jacket of a dark, grey cloth with decorative, braided buttons secured by braid loops. There was more decorative stitching on the cuffs and wide pockets with braided flaps over each hip. His dark trousers where thrust into black, buttoned boots.

As if to offset this sombre garb, the man's head was a shock of white hair, below which his brown and wrinkled face was thrown into sharp relief by the light from the lantern that he held high in his left hand.

Even Will was momentarily distracted by this Hammeresque apparition and it was a moment or two before he collected his thoughts, pulled his phone from his pocket and thumbed the menu.

We'd had no mobile signal since the first day of our holiday but, foreseeing possible difficulties in cycling through an alien land, we had researched and saved a selection of useful phrases before leaving the UK and it was a page of these that he now selected. 'Try one of those on him,' he instructed, handing me the instrument, fully aware of my immediate discomfort.

I scanned the list. 'Er, ne sunt ciclism si – au pierdut drumul nostru,' I intoned, and Will, recognising the lines, sniggered.

'We are cycling and have lost our way!' he translated, in mocking tones. 'I think Daisy, that given we are both on bicycles and standing in the dark half a mile from the nearest road, he's probably got that much already! Here let me have a go,' and he took the phone and, as he had perhaps always intended to do, took control too and with a beautifully inflected accent, asked, 'Ar putea gasi-ne o noapte de forbthe de pat?'

The old man regarded us thoughtfully and then gestured for us to step inside.

'What did you say?' I asked Will as we lifted our bikes over the low sill in the entranceway.

'I asked if he could find us a bed for the night,' he replied, 'and it looks as if we're on to a winner. Always trust your old mate William, my boy!'

I sighed and followed him across a cobbled yard, where the old man indicated we should leave our bikes, and then on up a flight of stone steps which led into a sombre hallway, from which a grander stairway disappeared into the upper gloom to left and right.

Unshouldering our backpacks we began the climb, the man looking back now and then to see that we were in tow. We eventually reached a landing from which a corridor led away into darkness for, by now, the only light came from the lantern. The walls were of peeling plaster, the floor, cracked tiles that formed ornate patterns beneath a coating of dust. Occasionally we passed a wall bracket that might have been intended for a torch or perhaps a candle. Everything reeked of age and decay, and disuse.

At a doorway the old man stopped, turned the handle and stood aside, waving us inside the revealed room. We entered and he followed. The interior was surprisingly well furnished with a respectable double bed and mattress. Opening the door to a closet the man pointed to neatly stored blankets and pillows. To the closet's left was an old but serviceable bathroom.

'Va multumesc,' I said. "Thank you" was one of the few Romanian phrases we had learned. The old man smiled for the first time and bowed slightly in response.

There was an awkward moment as the three of us stood, unsure of the next move and then an anxious look came over the old man's face and he pulled at my sleeve and moved towards the door.

Opposite our room a narrower stairway led up maybe a dozen steps to another doorway, this one intricately carved with stone vines and mythical creatures. The door itself was as solidly bound with iron fittings as the great gate outside and the timber looked furrowed with age.

Our host pointed to the door and spoke gravely for several minutes. I shook my head to indicate our lack of comprehension and he became agitated and, resorting to sign language, made it clear that we were not to climb the stairs and consequently not to

Countless times

enter the room beyond the door. On this he was emphatic, standing before the stairs and holding out his arms to bar the way, all the while shaking his head and grimacing wildly

Will grinned and said 'OK, OK' repeatedly until the old man seemed to accept that we understood, after which he lit candles from his lantern and placed them about our room. Then, with a final gesture towards the upper door and a furious shaking of his head, he left us and disappeared along the corridor.

'Oh My God!' roared Will, once we were completely alone, 'what...a...place! If this wasn't Bram Stoker's inspiration then I don't know what was! And what about Igor! He's straight out of Central Casting, isn't he?'

'Well, he's very elderly,' I ventured, 'so it's not surprising his clothes are a bit old fashioned.'

'Elderly? He's antediluvian! And the lantern? Oh, I love the lantern! Daisy, we are in Transylvania and alone, at night, in Count Dracula's castle! Don't that give you a tremor of apprehension, eh?' and he hunched one shoulder, contorted his face and extended his tongue.

'I think that's the Hunchback of Notre Dame,' I observed, pulling some bedclothes down from the shelf and tossing a pillow onto the mattress, 'we might as well get an early night, I don't think we'll be having a drink in the bar after a hearty dinner. Break open those fruit bars, it'll keep us going till we can find a café in the morning.'

'What do you think is in the room up the stairs?' said Will, ignoring my attempts at distraction, 'or should I say, who?'

'It's a private house Will,' I responded, 'he just doesn't want us poking around, is all. Now, make up your side of the bed.'

'I think Daisy is just an ickle bit nervous!' said Will, waving a finger at me in a ridiculously exaggerated manner. 'Do you think there might be someone hiding in the attic, Daisy?'

I glanced out through the open bedroom door at the shadowed stairway and traced the slight curve of the balustrade, up to the forbidden door. 'Don't be bloody ridiculous Will,' I said, suppressing the shiver which threatened to expose my foolishness.

'Or rather, someone *hidden*,' continued Will, enjoying the moment. 'That's more like it, eh? Hidden, not hiding: locked away to save the family from shame. Imprisoned at birth. Mad, or misshapen. Or...' he paused expecting me to prompt a continuation.

I obliged. 'Or what?' I had played this game with Will before.

'Or... inhuman.' He whispered the word into the silent confines of the room and refused to smile when I caught his eye. 'This isn't West Sussex, John, it's a lost tract of a foreign land that's a century adrift from the world outside. Down in the villages there are people who still believe in witchcraft; who lock their doors when the moon is full – it's true! - and you know it John, so don't show me that mocking face.'

I turned away and rummaged in my pack. I recognised this change of tone; the use of my proper name signalled the end of the joshing, the gentle teasing; what followed now would be more direct; a familiarity tinged with cruelty. I understood the psychology but I'd never learned to play the game.

'Pack it in, Will,' I muttered. Busying myself with my toiletries.

'Let's take a look,' said Will, suddenly decisive.

'A look?'

'In the room, John! You're not really afraid, are you?'

I bridled, 'Of course not, but it's none of our business.'

'Oh, but it is, Old Igor practically invited us up there! If he hadn't made such a fuss, we'd probably never have even noticed his wretched door. I think the old retainer protests too much!'

'Why the hell would he want two complete strangers - who I remind you arrived out of the blue - why would he want us poking around his home in the dark?'

'Ah, but that's just the point. He isn't the owner. Like I said, he's the retainer and maybe there's something he's desperate to reveal but can't bring himself to tell us upfront.'

'And maybe he sees us as the next blood donors for his employer, who'll be climbing out of his coffin any time now and feeling peckish,' I snapped, regretting my sarcasm before I had completed the sentence.

'Now who's being ridiculous?' said Will, quietly.

I found my toothpaste and dropped it into the bag with my brush. 'Well then,' I said, after a minute had passed.

'Well then,' repeated Will, 'we might as well get it done with, and then we can go to bed. Are you coming?'

'For Christ's sake Will,' I said resignedly, 'let's do it.'

He smiled for the only time since he'd used my name and, rounding the bed, placed his am across my back and gripped my arm encouragingly, like a team captain, sending in his last batsman, with six required for a win.

Side by side we crossed the passageway and mounted the stairs until we stood before the mysterious doorway and I ran my finger over the incised creatures that decorated the portal. Close to, they resembled no animals real or imagined that I had ever encountered; and there were other figures, semi-human, with devils' faces and oddly scaled limbs. All entwined with stone-cut leaves and ropes.

The door by comparison was rustically plain; huge planks of grey oak, without adornment, other than that provided by the hinges and a great iron hoop of a handle, which hung from the grasping teeth of another imaginary beast.

'Want to do the honours?' said Will, pointing to this last.

I hesitated, looked back down towards the corridor, half hoping we would be discovered, and then reached out tentatively and grasped the circle of iron.

As I did so, deep within the room beyond the door something groaned and I snatched back my hand

Countless times

and stumbled away, down the stairway to the sanctuary of our own bedroom door where I stood, half screened by the frame looking back in barely concealed terror.

At the stairs' crest, Will looked down and laughed silently at my plight. 'Oh, Daisy,' he exclaimed, 'you really are such a girl,' and then he turned back, wrenched the door open and stepped boldly into the blackness of the interior.

His scream was the most terrible sound I ever heard and though it lasted for only seconds, its echo still disturbs my sleep, though years have passed since then.

The old man, who was the owner of the house, was distraught beyond measure. He had known of the danger and had tried his best to warn us, but his natural courtesy and the demands of hospitality that his culture placed upon him had over-ridden such considerations. His society was out of time. They left their doors unfastened and found it difficult to imagine that guests might disregard their own obligations of gratitude and respect. We sought shelter and it could not be refused, even though he would never have chosen to invite us to stay. He was old and his wealth was lost with the war and his home falling into ruin. The door at the top of the stairs opened into a tower infested with woodworm and rot and my sometimes friend had fallen four floors to his unnecessary death.

Through a glass, darkly

Kate had visited the witch before. In a world beset by dark forces and evil humours her charms and potions allayed fears and cooled fevers; a firepowder to frighten away chimney ghouls; an infusion of juniper for a toothache. Life was fragile and the world was filled with snares and dark mysteries. Pain and distress were all around but for those who knew its secrets, the Earth provided. Herbs and roots; saps and berries; powders and unguents. The witch concocted remedies for human ailments and talismans to protect against the devil and his minions.

And some said that the flame-haired woman possessed even more arcane knowledge; deep magic that transgressed the church's otherwise grudging acceptance of her presence; powers which placed her in the uncertain shadow lands that flickered between good and evil; a command over life and death that scared the priest into silence.

Kate knew of these stories and they added a cautious respect to her demeanour as she descended the steps from the alley and pushed open the ironbound door into the witch's parlour.

The bright day flooded into the gloom of the interior, lighting the dusty beams festooned with their bunches of dried leaves and flowers, and then, as the door swung closed behind her, the wide patch

Through a glass darkly

of sunlight quickly narrowed as it ran across the shelves of jars and books until, for a second, it became a single, thin column of illumination before vanishing suddenly into complete darkness. In that briefest of moments before the light was extinguished, Kate thought she saw a flash of auburn hair; a glint of teeth in a sharp smile; a green eye reflecting her own, startled, face.

Kate had come to the witch seeking only a remedy for her husband's infidelity, not a punishment. When she had finally understood that his restless and unhappy manner was a symptom of an emotional turmoil and that his wordless departures took him, not to the solace of the local inn but to the arms of a lover, it had evinced not jealousy but an overwhelming sense of grief and loss. Her urgent need was to return things to the way they had been; to clear his memory of her rival's face, her rival's body.

In her despair she remembered the witch and placed a desperate confidence in the woman's ability to restore her lost love: a subtle mix of plants and liquors, a recipe to influence the conflicting passions.

Now, she stood in the darkness and held her breath, waiting for her heart-beat to slow. Around her there was utter stillness. She recalled the room and the shuttered window and turning to her right, reached out to open it. Fumbling along the wall she realised she was mistaken; the window must be to the left of the door. She stepped across, found the hinged, wooden cover and pulled it towards her.

A dim light filtered into the room through the horn panels. She turned and surveyed the parlour.

There was something different about the room that was hard to understand. It was still dominated, as on her previous visits, by the huge oak table, on which bowls and dishes were neatly stacked. One wall was covered by shelves; rows of ornate, blue ceramic jars filled some, whilst others were home to large, glass containers within which, strange, vaguely organic shapes slowly coiled and twisted. On a low bench a row of peeling, leather-bound volumes shared space with a large pestle and mortar and to one side a metal brazier held the cold remains of a fire which had spilled its ash onto the flagstone floor. An archway, which might have formed the entrance to rooms beyond, was draped with a woollen rug, tied back with an elaborate sash, and on the further wall was the mirror.

It had excited Kate's attention the first time she had called on the witch. Mirrors were rare and valuable items and it was the only glass one which she had ever seen. It was hung as a picture would be hung and was an arm's length in width and half as high. The glass was cloudy with its edges pocked and grey and the frame was pitted, cracked ebony, carved into intricate patterns of knots and spirals.

Kate frowned as she examined the room's reflection. She was sure that on her earlier visits the mirror had hung on the opposite wall. She could clearly remember that it was the first thing in view as she entered, pushing the door to the right. She looked back at the door. It was hinged to swing left.

Through a glass darkly

With growing fear she re-examined her surroundings; the shelves, the arch, the bench; they were all transposed.

She ran to the mirror, an awful realisation forming in her mind, and stared into its imperfect surface. In the room beyond, the furniture and fittings were as she recalled them; the window on the right, the curtained opening to the left. As she watched, the rug was pulled aside and the witch stepped into the reflected room and looked towards the door. Kate shot a look over her shoulder; her room was empty but back in the mirror the door was opening and a figure was entering and reaching out to the witch.

As her husband and his red-headed lover fell into each other's arms, Kate pressed her face and hands hard against the mirror's face and screamed into it, not ceasing even when she realised she had no reflection and that the couple were alone on their side of the glass.

Mortal, invisible

The Reverend John Tregain closed the door quietly and stood in the cool dusk surveying the cobbled stable yard and, through the open gates, the distant smudge of moorland. At his back, The Manor was a dark wall of granite, offering no comfort or compassion to his troubled heart.

'He's alive! John, he's alive!' An hour earlier Merryn had stood on the steps of the old house, red hair framing her radiant features, one hand waving the letter that was to destroy his hopes and plunge its recipient into madness.

Alive? It couldn't be; it was too long. No news of the ship or any of its crew for two years and more. No word from the family's estates. Taken by Atlantic storms, that's what the sailors said, down at the dock.

Even so, the vicar had framed his features into a semblance of hopeful anticipation and suppressed the wave of despair that her words had triggered.

The letter, when he examined it, was in a hand like enough to that of Merryn's husband but its content was wild and Godless.

'It's a cruel joke!' he had told her, afraid that his relief must show in his eyes, 'you must see that. This is the stuff of nightmares and superstition.

Mortal, invisible

Daniel is dead, you can't set store by this – the product of some delirious crewmember.'

To begin with the narrative was plausible, if extraordinary. It told of shipwreck on a bleak headland of the island of Monserrat and capture by a group of runaway slaves, of strange rites and drug-induced hallucinations. It described an attempted escape and, in its course, the death of a native and a terrible reprisal in which all the crew, save for the letter's author, was put to death. For Daniel Pengelly, the slave-master, a more dreadful fate was in store: he had been cursed, by a pagan priestess, to roam the Earth as a living ghost. Not dead but without substance; part of this world but unseen by his fellow men, until at last he died on that same distant isle.

'But in that, at least, the curse has been broken, for he has sent this letter on ahead, to prepare me for his arrival,' said Merryn, and there was an absolute conviction in her voice as she added, 'soon, Daniel and I will be reunited.'

Tregain was a man of God; he did not believe the tale of an invisible man but it mattered not to him whether it be true or false; in either case the woman he had always loved was lost to him and all he could do now was watch over her in her derangement and protect her from the perpetrator of the hoax - for he was sure that the letter came from someone who had known Daniel and who intended to seek some advantage from the situation.

Whines & spirits

He walked across the yard to where his horse waited patiently, its breath steaming in the chill October evening. As he reached for the reigns, there was a disturbance in the air, a shifting of the leaves scattered across the cobbles and, as he swung around scanning the empty courtyard, the door to The Manor eased closed with what might have been the movement of the passing breeze.

Tregain called at The Manor often after that evening and on each occasion he found Merryn more deeply immersed in her delusion, more convinced than ever that she shared her home with an unseen man whom the troubled vicar knew was surely dead.

'He will not make his presence known to you, John,' she told him once, 'he believes you would be troubled by the revelation that such things are possible.'

Tregain dismissed such claims, sure of a different motive for the letter which had unbalanced her mind but although he kept a careful eye on strangers in the village and on vagrants crossing the path across the moor, he never found reason to suspect that any had designs on Merryn or her possessions and, as the years passed, he forgot his suspicions and remembered only that he had once loved the mad old woman who lived at the granite house on the edge of the moor.

Mortal, invisible

On New Year's Eve, in the Year of our Lord, 1759, the Reverend John Tregain arrived at the imposing front door of The Manor and, finding it open despite the snow which dusted its ledges and brass fittings, stepped inside and made about to call out for the mistress of the house. It was at that very moment that he heard a shriek from the direction of the great hall and throwing down his hat but retaining his gloves and overcoat he hurried, as fast as his now aging frame could manage, across the hallway and onto the threshold of that room. He was met by Merryn herself, grey hair dishevelled, a look of dismay on her lined but still handsome features. At sight of the priest she let out a piercing wail and clutched at his coat, which was damp from the melting snow.

'Murder! Murder! Daniel is murdered by this thief who has broken into our home!' and she pointed back into the hall where a stooped figure stood beside the fireplace.

As Tregain hurried forward he could see that the man was elderly, white haired and bearded and dressed in a threadbare assortment of old clothes.

'What are you doing here, n'er-do-well!' roared the vicar, taking up a poker from the hearth and brandishing it in the face of the tramp. 'Explain your behaviour this instant! If you've injured this lady you'll pay with your life!'

'John, John, it's me,' replied the man, raising a hand in a token of defence, 'the curse has been lifted; I am made visible once more.'

Whines & spirits

'Lies! Lies!' screeched Merryn, from the doorway, 'do you think I would not know my Daniel, fool? You have killed him and hidden his body, Oh, what will I do without him?'

Tregain stared at the scene in horror. What he had once feared had come to pass. The rogue who had set up this hoax so long ago had come to claim his inheritance! Why he had left it so long Tregain could only surmise: enough years for Merryn's dementia to fog her mind? Time for age to disguise his features? Whatever the plan, he had forced his way into the manor and was threatening the woman for whom, regardless of her ruined mind, Tregain still felt a lasting love. With the rage of a lifetime's denial, Tregain swung the poker and brought his rival to the ground.

Merryn left The Manor that day and never returned, spending the rest of her days in the asylum. The tramp survived Tregain's attack but stood trial. With no body to be found and no expectation of finding one either, there could be no accusation of murder but he was found guilty of breaking and entering and of attempted theft, for which he was sentenced to deportation and penal servitude in the British colony of Monserrat. When news came of his death there, a few years later, John Tregain remembered the curse and its prediction and he wondered if the tramp really could have been Daniel Pengelly and whether he had wondered the same thing, back in the hall, when he had wielded the poker.

Just desserts

Lee jumped down from the stile and stood, hands resting on his knees as he recovered his breath. There was no sound of pursuit, no voices raised in concern, just the course cry of a rook winging its way to the distant copse through the darkening sky.

He bared his teeth in a mirthless smile and pulled up the zip of his coat. It was already chilly, his breath clouding the air as he set off across the field. He could come out on Garbitt's Lane and make his way back to the village along the main road, to the pub. There was a darts match on tonight and, when he joined the crowd in the bar, no one would be any the wiser about his earlier stroll through the churchyard and what he'd done there.

The path through the field was overgrown and difficult to make out as the light faded into night. It was some sort of crop, which at first, he could not distinguish. There were large dark shapes among a tangle of foliage and when his hurrying feet caught in the trailing vines he stumbled and fell heavily among them.

They were pumpkins: fat-stalked, rough-leaved and, when he levered himself upright, he saw that they stretched off, row after row, dull orange fading into shadow.

Lee understood nothing of the farmer's imperatives regarding such a harvest but he was not

Just desserts

indifferent to the fruit's associations with the celebration of Hallowe'en and a familiar memory stirred in his subconscious and sent a shiver through his slight frame.

He'd been disturbed by the churchyard, too; afterwards. After he'd pulled the girl's body into the shrubbery and run to the lychgate to ensure that the lane was empty. He'd looked back at the crowded tombstones and the brooding presence of the church tower, and a concern, not for what he'd done but for what the consequences might be, had filled his ears with the sound of his own blood. And he'd run then; past the sightless, accusing angels and the carved crosses raised in exorcism at his awful intrusion; run till the pounding in his veins had threatened to burst his heart, as his ma had always warned him it could, back when he was a kid and she took him for those visits to the medic.

"Congenital," that's what they'd called it and she'd blamed his dad, who Lee had never known, and then she'd died herself of "heart failure", because that's what the doctor had written on her death certificate. And after that Lee hadn't known who to blame and he'd never been back to the hospital.

Now he stood among the pumpkins and turned towards the village, where the church and its brooding yew were still silhouetted against the last, ice blue shard of sky, and he thought of the girl under the shroud of rhododendrons.

Gabrielle Broom, stupid little slut! Been desperate for it, to start with. Worked him up like, then screamed for him to stop and that's when he'd seen

Whines & spirits

red. Just cos 'er family owned Meadows Farm, she thought she was better'n he was. So, it weren't 'is fault, not really, were it?

As he watched, the last trace of day drained from the sky and the night folded around him, complete, and the first stars came on, cold and sharp and he swung round and set off through the pumpkins and tried to think of something else; and the pumpkins whispered to him in the cold, frosting air and he remembered - though he pushed the memory back - he remembered his first Hallowe'en and his brother Gary.

Lee had only been about seven, and Gary maybe twelve, and they'd left their bedroom that October thirty-one and climbed down into the bottomless pit below their window, where Gary said the ghostly Pumpkin Man was waiting to gather boys into his black, twiggy arms. And, even at seven, Lee had only half believed, until Gary had vanished and left him alone in the invisible garden.

He'd done his best to hold himself together; put his back to the wall and fought to control his trembling limbs, and maybe he'd have been alright if the Pumpkin Man hadn't suddenly shouted his name and appeared with his monstrous, orange head and spindly, spidery hands.

That was the night they'd found out about his heart and Gary had been brought to his hospital bed and made to say he was sorry and Lee had been too tired to care.

The field seemed to be endless. He'd lost the path and was using the starlight's faint illumination of

Just desserts

the distant hills as a guide. Somewhere, off to the east, the moon was rising behind a bank of cloud and a thin line of silver showed at its edge. By now he must be nearing the lane. A smudge of hedgerows appeared to left and right; a slight paling suggested an opening and he moved towards it.

Suddenly, the moon broke free of the cloud cover and the whole nightscape was bathed in a grey/blue light. In comparison to the impenetrable gloom which had preceded it, the moonlight rendered the scene in vivid contrasts: deep shadows and bright highlights.

Lee stopped, momentarily disorientated by the change and, as he stood before the now clearly defined gate, a figure reared up from among the pumpkins and stood before him. It was tall and lean and atop its shoulders was a huge, bloated orange head.

Lee's eyes widened, his pulse set up a staccato beat in his wrists, his heart hammered at his ribs, and then the night went black once more and his lifeless body dropped among the rough leaves.

Edward Broom settled the pumpkin more comfortably on his shoulder and continued towards the gate. Tomorrow the rest of the crop would be harvested but this prize example would take pride of place over the entrance to Meadows Farm. He'd set Gabrielle to carving it, just as soon as she returned from organ practice at the church.

The hand

'Uncle had never believed any of the stories associated with the hand, up to the moment when he moved back to Alverstone,' I told Vicky, as we explored the library of the ancient building, on that first afternoon after I took possession.

'So what changed his mind?' she asked, walking round the dusty display case in order to view its ghastly contents from every angle.

'Nothing,' I replied, joining her to peer in at the shrivelled remains. 'As far as I know it was nothing more than a sort of melodramatic gesture to show his frustration about all that had happened. He didn't expect a response.

'Of course, Great Aunt Cissie didn't see it that way; she was quite sure that his actions would lead to disaster. "You can't toy with the occult," she told him, and when he scoffed at what he called her "foolish delusions," she just looked at him with a kind of despairing pity and said, "I just pray that you live to prove they are merely that." '

'Come on then,' insisted Vicky, throwing herself into one of the library's green velvet, deep-buttoned armchairs, 'you were here when it happened, tell me the whole story.'

The hand

I sighed and lowered myself into the chair on the opposite side of the great, oak-framed fireplace. 'Do you believe in ghosts?' I began.

It was November and late afternoon; the light had already faded from the sky, turning the windows' leaded panes into black, diamond mirrors which caught and reflected the leaping flames from the hearth, and they, in turn, threw jerky shadows into the casements' deep recesses and transformed the curtains' heavy folds into textured pillars lost in the darkness of the high ceilings. It was such a night and such a setting that the most practical of women might have been excused a moment of doubt but Vicky merely laughed.

'Of course I don't, Bamber! This is the twenty-first century you know. I appreciate that your family can trace itself back to the Stone Age and that they used some of those stones to build Alverstone Abbey but old doesn't mean creepy – not in my book. It just means rising damp and no cavity wall insulation! I'm sorry,' she added, 'I didn't mean to spoil your story; please carry on.'

'Well, Uncle Harry would probably have expressed his feelings in much the same way,' I conceded, 'when he first inherited the family home. After all, he was a no-nonsense army man, not given to flights of fancy. That's why he tried so hard to find a rational explanation for what happened here, in the first few weeks following his arrival.

'It started in small, almost unnoticed ways. An insignificant object apparently mislaid and found later in an unexpected place; a chair left awkwardly

Whines & spirits

in a doorway; a teatime treat missing from the larder. I'm afraid Uncle blamed the lady from the village who came in to do the cleaning and that resulted in her handing in her notice and a deal of resentment from the local community.

'It wasn't old Harry's finest hour but being alone was instructive because the odd occurrences didn't end with the domestic's departure; in fact, they intensified.

'There was nothing you could say was overtly sinister or even identifiably supernatural. The bath water running freezing cold might have been a plumbing fault – although the plumber could identify no deficiency with the boiler system. The wide window that let in the rain on a stormy night and ruined a hall table, could have been a faulty catch – 'though no fault was discernible. The locked door, which slammed loudly at midnight and was discovered still locked, perhaps had secured itself on impact with the frame – even if it was difficult to explain how the bolts were also shot. Hardly a day went by without some incident that resulted in inconvenience and annoyance.

'And then things got more serious. A huge masonry urn fell from the roofline moments after a visitor had passed and smashed itself and the paving into fragments. An urgent examination of the structure found no decay, no erosion to account for the event but an explanation was in the offing, never the less, because the visitor was Great Aunt Cissie and she declared the culprit to be a poltergeist.'

The hand

'A poltergeist?' Vicky grinned and her teeth caught the firelight's gleam.

'A poltergeist!' I grinned back, 'once again Uncle Harry's response was much the same as yours.'

' "A poltergeist," Great Aunt Cissie had insisted. "It's no surprise, surely you know that the Abbey has been haunted for generations?"

' "No,' replied Uncle firmly. "Oh, I've heard plenty of tales, naturally, but I don't accept a word of 'em. It's all bloody nonsense, if you'll excuse my French. When you're dead, you're dead and you can't come back to heave bloody great chunks of Portland stone at people – no matter how aggravating they might be," he added pointedly.

' "Well, of course," continued my Great Aunt, unabashed, "It all started with the old Abbot who delved into black magic and devil worship back in the thirteenth century. Only God knows what poor souls met their ends at his hands. And speaking of hands, you have seen it I suppose?"

' "Oh, I've seen the hand alright," replied Uncle, "it's not something you're likely to miss, is it? A severed, mummified hand, in a glass jar. Most people make do with a vase from Ikea."

' "It's a hanged man's hand," said Cissie, "cut from a corpse while the blood was still warm. They believed it could grant wishes, but only the unwise tested its efficacy." '

'Why did she say that?' asked Vicky, interested despite her earlier derision of all things supernatural.

Whines & spirits

'The old warning of being careful what you ask for,' I explained. 'In case,' I added, 'your wish comes true.' She looked puzzled by that but didn't respond so I continued with my narrative.

'Next day a faulty switch nearly electrocuted me – oh, I should explain that I'd arrived by this time; the family were having one of their annual get-togethers. I survived but I had some nasty burns on my fingers. Still, the final straw was Uncle Harry's car. The brakes failed as he was coming down the steep part of the drive and he careered into the stable wall. It did quite a lot of damage to the wall and the car, and Uncle was incandescent.

'He stormed into the library, where we were all gathered awaiting his return and he bellowed, "I don't pretend to understand what's going on but yesterday it was Cissie, this morning it was young Bamber and five minutes ago I was nearly done for in the car. Oh, I don't suppose there's any point in having the wiring checked, do you? - or the brakes for that matter. Cissie? You say it's a ghost? Well, I say this. If I get my hands on the bloody ghost it'll wish it had stayed in the nether regions..."

'You can't "get your hands on a ghost," Uncle,' I interrupted, in an attempt to lighten the mood a little, 'it's not a practical proposition!'

But he wasn't to be mollified. He strode over to that ghastly hand, pulled off the cover and grabbed those awful waxy digits in his own and he waved it in the air and shouted, "I want to deal with that ghost, do you hear me? You're supposed to grant wishes, well grant me this." It was all amateur

The hand

dramatics of course. Like I said, he didn't believe a word of Great Aunt Cissie's story, he just wanted to let off steam. Next morning, he was dead.'

For long minutes there was silence in the room. The fire had burned down and I stood and threw a log onto the embers. A shower of sparks leapt into the chimney space and I took up the poker and prodded the lifeless wood until a flame began to lick up around it once more.

'He got up in the night, probably because he heard sounds of movement, and in the dark he fell over a low, ironbound chest that had been dragged across the landing. There were thirteen steps to the next turn of the stairs and that was where we found him, his neck broken by the fall.'

I stood, warming myself and looked down at Vicky to gauge her reaction.

'Poor old sod!' she said, 'although, in a way, his death proved what a load of cobblers the whole haunted house story was. I mean, he didn't last long enough to have his wish granted, did he?'

'Next night,' I said, without commenting on her dismissal of Aunt Cissie's claims, 'the whole family were woken by the sounds of a terrible fight but though we searched the house we could find no intruders, no sign of disturbance.'

'And...'

'And after that the poltergeist was never heard from again. No more accidents or incidents, to this day.'

'So, no ghosts in Alverstone Abbey!' said Vicky with satisfaction, 'makes it conveniently difficult to prove anything ever happened, doesn't it?'

'No ghosts?' I said, 'I never told you that. You know, there's only one thing that can get its hands on a ghost and that's another ghost, so perhaps Uncle Harry had his wish granted after all. In which case,' I concluded, 'once he'd seen off the poltergeist, he would have had the Abbey all to himself. Maybe you'll bump into him when you make your way up to bed tonight!'

Night shift

'Fancy a cuppa?' asked Jed, opening cupboards at random until his search finally revealed the crockery for which he was searching.

'Er, no, no I won't thanks,' replied the mansion's only other occupant, 'I'd better be getting back to my wiring if I'm going to get the job finished.'

'Come on!' urged Jed, locating the tea bags and casting around for the sugar. 'Drinking a mug of...' he paused and rotated the packet in his left hand to display the product details, '...Earl Grey - hey there's posh - well, it won't delay the grand opening, will it?'

'I suppose not,' said the other, doubtfully, 'if you're looking for company.'

'Well, it's going to be a long old night,' observed Jed, flicking the switch on the kettle and setting out on a new quest, for biscuits, 'now that Nick's cried off with man-flu.'

'And are you really looking for ghosts?' The electrician had pulled up a stool and was watching as Jed rummaged among a promising collection of bags and boxes below the working top.

'Ha! Chocolate Hobnobs!' Jed held up his quarry triumphantly. 'Well, Nick is. He's the believer, I'm only his bag carrier.' He climbed to his feet, placed the biscuits on the centre of the table and turned back to the kettle, which was whistling, fractiously.

Night shift

'Actually, that not quite true – the bit about him being a believer. He'd insist that he's agnostic when it comes to the question of the afterlife. No, that's not right either. Here, hang on a mo while I pour this tea. I'll let you add your own milk and stuff.'

He pushed one of the mugs across to his companion and tore open the biscuits' wrapper so that the contents spilled onto the table. Then he dragged over a second stool and settled himself, hands enfolding his own mug, elbows supporting his thin frame as he leaned into the rising wisp of steam and took a sip.

'The paranormal, that's what Nick calls it, stuff "which is beyond the range of normal experience or scientific explanation," to quote him word for word. And he'd tell you that as an investigator, he neither believes in nor doubts the existence of, anything "supernatural". He'd say, and I know, 'cos I've had this conversation with him myself, that electricity was beyond the range of normal experience or scientific explanation once upon a time, but that didn't mean it was magic or occult. It just needed investigation and explanation.'

Jed paused and bit into a Hobnob with obvious satisfaction before wiping the crumbs from his mouth and adding, 'on the other hand, anyone who spends their nights staking out supposedly haunted houses trying to make contact with spooks, can't be effing normal, can they?' and he grinned conspiratorially.

'See, I'm good with electronics and remotes and so Nick got me on board to handle the technical

Whines & spirits

gizmos. That's why we...I'm, going ahead tonight, regardless. Anyone can gather gen, and that's what I'll be doing. I've got temperature sensors, infra-red cameras, high and low frequency sound recorders and some even more fancy stuff and between you and me, I could head for home and a good night's kip but Nick insists on the personal touch. He says the finest array of sensory equipment is built-in to the human body so, whatever high-tech gubbins we use, we still need to observe, personally. And that's because the real area under investigation is the interface between the haunted and whatever's doing the haunting. Nick says, "Think Jed, what is it that's frightening someone who's alone, in the dark, in a house that ISN'T haunted?"

'Nick thinks things like that, which is probably why he's the boss and I'm the bottle-washer! He's quite famous, you know, in the world of the paranormal; that's how he got hired by this place's new owner, to give it the once over. He's Chinese, the owner, and dead chuffed to think he's buying a genuine, haunted, English house. Apparently, it'll add to his prestige with his friends back home.

'Right, better get to battle stations, eh? Where are you working?'

'In the long, upstairs corridor.'

'Well, don't short anything out and set the curtains alight - there's no fire escape from the first floor! Look, seriously, I'll be making myself comfortable out in the hall, at the bottom of the stairs. If you see or hear anything unusual, give me a shout and I'll

Night shift

come running, OK? I'd love to come up with something Nick can't explain for once!

He watched as the electrician gathered his tool bag, climbed the wide staircase and disappeared into the oak-panelled gloom. It was twelve-thirty and time to douse the lights. He threw the switch and waited while his eyes adjusted to the darkness, then he lowered himself into a deep leather armchair beside the rising balustrade. On a table before him the screen of the tiny monitor caste a thin, green light, which illuminated nothing but the table's edge. Somewhere to his left, an unseen clock ticked ponderously. Above him, at the stairs' head, a pale luminescence waxed and waned, evidence he supposed of the electrician's activities in the distant corridor.

Jed yawned, felt around beside the chair and found the paperback he had brought to fill the hours of waiting. He switched on the book-light clipped to its dog-eared cover and settled back. You had to wonder, he confessed to himself, who was the most deluded. Nick, who, despite his insistence on rationality and the scientific method was surely seeking some sort of spiritual revelation or Jed himself who believed in none of it and yet dedicated fruitless hours of inactivity to its cause - the single advantage being the almost guaranteed intrigue aroused in girls who had been incautious enough to ask him what he did for a living. He smiled in the darkness and opened the book at Chapter Three.

Time passed.

Suddenly, something brought him to full alertness. He sat stiffly, listening into the silence, then carefully re-clipped the reading light above the introduction to Chapter Fifteen and switched off the power.

The clock had stopped. The house was temporarily unoccupied and the mechanism had not been wound. How odd that the absence of sound should have disturbed him so effectively.

He stood and stretched, squinting out into the empty hall, the accoutrements of which were now delineated by a wane moonlight filtered through scudding clouds and dusty diamond panes. Time perhaps to make a round of the other instruments.

At the top of the stairs he paused and scrutinised the passageway ahead. It was hidden in almost impenetrable darkness; no sign of the electrician or the light by which he must surely be working.

Jed edged forward, arms waving slowly from side to side to detect obstacles in his path. At the junction with the transverse corridor he stopped again before a wide latticed window and looked left and right and, as he did so, the moon cleared the clouds and revealed to either side, three closed doors.

He stepped to his left, remaining half-turned to keep the rest of the corridor in view, tried each door and found it locked. He walked across to the right-hand arm, repeated his action with the first two doors and elicited the same result. The remaining door was at right angles to the others and, as he

Night shift

reached for the handle and found it yielded to his touch, the moon was again eclipsed by cloud.

As the door swung slowly, slowly inwards, the sparse light failed and left him blind on the threshold, and as he fought to quell the primeval, instinctive fear of the dark, a shrill and terrifying sound cut suddenly through his whole being and, in an instant, he was drenched in his own sweat.

'Jesus, Nick!' He dragged the phone from his inside pocket, thumbed the receive button and shouted obscenities at his absent employer. 'I nearly had a coronary!' He stood, the phone pressed to his ear, his breathing in rapid step with his heartbeat.

'Hello Jed,' he could hear a note of amusement in the voice, 'didn't think you were scared of ghosts! I didn't wake you up, I hope. How's it going down there?'

Jed waited while his breathing came under control. The moon had reappeared and bathed the almost empty room before him.

'No,' he answered, trying to sound indignant at both suggestions, 'everything's fine, as it happens; the usual no-show on the ghost front. What am I supposed to be looking for this time, by the way? A headless cavalier? A woman in white?' He rotated slowly, examining every corner of the room. Where the hell was that guy doing the wiring? The only way out of the house had been down the stairs and Jed knew that no one had passed his chair in over three hours.

'No need for sarcasm, Jed,' Nick's voice had

Whines & spirits

adopted a more didactic tone, 'not all paranormal sightings are of characters from the long past. As a matter of fact, the event which brought about claims of haunting at the manor only took place twenty or so years ago.'

Jed walked to the centre of the room and looked down at the object that lay there.

'Quite mundane, in way,' continued Nick, 'a workman modernising the place electrocuted himself.'

'Nick,' said Jed, quietly, as he knelt and examined the bag of tools, 'you're not going to believe this.'

The house in the wood

Mary carefully lowered her armful of bowls and beakers onto the sand in the shallows beside the cascade and then stepped across to a wide, flat rock at the edge of the tumbling water. She reached back, took one of the vessels and scooped it into the sand, swirling it round and round to scour the surface. Then she turned and washed it clean in the foaming stream.

She hated the chore and knew that Evlan appointed her to the task for that very reason, relishing her younger sister's discomfort. Mary could not protest; her father adhered strictly to the codes of rank and servitude and to disobey would have brought her shame and punishment. But the woods ringing the pool at the foot of the falls were a place of deep shadows and uncertain movements and sometimes there were sounds, unfamiliar and disturbing sounds, like children crying out in despair.

Alun said that it was only the sound of ravens, squabbling in the branches of the twisted, moss-covered oaks, which grew amongst the split, grey boulders on the slopes below the village. Mary knew he was trying to comfort her but she knew too that

The house in the wood

neither he nor any of his brothers would go far into the stunted forest and that he was grateful that boys were not called on to clean dishes.

Today, there was a silence beneath the dark trees and the air was still and heavy in contrast to the ceaseless noise and motion of the small river where the sunlight sparked on the splashing water like the tiny, bright stars that fell from her father's fire-flint.

As she cleaned each item, she stacked it safely where the current reversed and formed a quiet eddy among the slick, round stones. When she finished the last bowl, she stood and stretched the muscles in her legs. First the right, then the left and, as she did so, the rock on which she had been squatting, moved in the gravel and rotated under her foot. She fought for her balance and fell forward, her hands sinking into the gritty silt. As she righted herself, she saw with consternation that the rock's movement had altered the water's flow and toppled the bowls. The uppermost had floated free and was being carried into the centre of the stream.

With a small cry she grabbed at the rest of the receptacles and pushed them out, onto the sand, then she swung back to recover the loose bowl. It was already some feet away and moving into deeper water. She lifted her feet, pulled off her sandals and threw them to the shore. The pebbles were smooth but they were loose and she almost fell again as she paddled forward. Suddenly she was up to her thighs. The cold made her catch her breath but she plunged on, reaching for the bowl as it bobbed away

Whines & spirits

to where the surface flattened and the reflections dimmed and the river entered the wood.

As the current dragged her down, Mary saw the bowl dip, fill and, losing equilibrium, sink. Then she too went down into the glass green waters, trailing bubbles, eyes screwed shut.

The hollow was small and when she thrashed her way back into the light, she could already feel the bottom scratching against her bare toes. But the gradient had increased and she was powerless to halt her progress, at one moment floating free and fast and at the next slewing against giant boulders and bumping over small stones. The banks rushed past in a blur of bramble and bark, as fast as a hunting dog could run and, as the river straightened, her speed increased, carrying her further and further from her home. Then, all at once, she was falling; falling until her body smacked into something hard and her breath was carried away.

When she regained control of her lungs she laid, gulping in the air and listening to the roar all around her.

After a while she raised herself, painfully, struggling against the deluge, and found that she was on a flat shelf of rock at the base of a small waterfall.

The rocky crag over which the river fell, circled off to each side, tapering in height as it went. Moving carefully, Mary was able to climb up and out of the defile and into a sunny clearing formed by a fallen

The house in the wood

oak, now no more than a jumble of branches among the grass.

She could see nothing around her but the forest. In one direction the ground rose towards her now distant village and in the other, it continued to descend, carrying the river with it.

She found the fallen tree's trunk and sat down to consider her situation. The day was hot and her thin summer smock was already drying but her feet were bare and a long climb back over the rugged, pathless hillside seemed an impossible task. Except, she thought, examining the undergrowth on one side of the clearing, maybe it wasn't pathless after all. There was a narrow trail there where the grass did not grow quite as tall. It was not much more than a shadow among the leaves and stems but it was something. Perhaps it was an animal track but were the creatures that made it, wild or domesticated? That thought brought her up, sharp. Her old fear had been forgotten for a while as she dealt with the more immediate concerns of her perilous river journey. Now, the horror of her situation burst in on her. She was in the heart of the forest which every member of her community shunned; a place that was referred to in hushed whispers and harsh curses; home of wolves and bears and, some said, lost spirits.

Mary shivered despite the sun and leaping to her feet ran to the trail. Any action was better than sitting and waiting for one of the denizens of the wood to find her.

Whines & spirits

The path, if that's what it was, soon led into the trees but although it was sometimes obscured by tangled roots and occasionally cut through by runnels of rust brown water, it never disappeared altogether and eventually, it took Mary to the house.

Agrid saw the old building before she found the lost goat. Its shape loomed up amongst the trees and, when she stepped out onto the patch of beaten earth that led up to its door, she discovered the animal chewing unconcernedly on a sow thistle at the edge of the path.

Agrid was not a nervous girl; if she had been, she would never have followed the errant member of her flock into the forest. She was however, aware of the woodland's reputation and she exercised an appropriate caution as she circled the dwelling and reached out to slip a rope around the goat's neck.

Still, she did not hear the door open and it was only as she turned to retrace her steps, that she became aware of a figure standing there, watching her, silently.

Agrid poised, ready for flight, even prepared to abandon the goat if necessary, although the danger would have to very great for her to consider that.

She relaxed a little when she realised that the eyes regarding her so intently were those of a young girl, of about her own age. She was wearing a simple light smock, despite the winter's chill, and her feet were bare.

The house in the wood

'Are you from the village?' the girl asked, and before Agrid could answer she added, 'I thought that Alun might come to find me.'

'I was searching for the animal,' replied Agrid, inclining her head towards the beast, which had pulled away and resumed its meal of thistle. 'But, yes, I am from the village.'

The girl did not respond immediately and Agrid appraised her thoughtfully. She knew of only one man named Alun in the village and he was her grandfather. What possible circumstance could connect the two?

The girl took a step back, into the cottage's dark interior and beckoned for Agrid to follow. Agrid, her curiosity aroused, did so.

'My name,' said the girl, closing the door behind them, 'is Mary,' and, there in the shadows, she smiled for the first time as Agrid's eyes widened in terror.

Mary was a name no villager could choose for her child. The Elder had forbidden its use long before Agrid had been born. He had forbidden too that the Teller of Tales, should weave any stories about the daughter he had lost and Agrid had noticed that whenever a younger member of her own family questioned this injunction, her grandfather silenced them and became lost in his own thoughts.

But even as she remembered these things they slipped from her mind, as the light faded in the woods beyond the window.

Mary moved past her towards an inner door and Agrid felt the dampness of her dress against her arm before the door swung open and the girls turned towards it.

'Come and meet the others,' said Mary and her smile showed bone-white in the shadows.

The sexton

The Reverend Thaddeus McClaver dipped his head in a silent goodnight and quietly closed the cottage door on the fire's glow and the small group clustered about the bed. For a moment he stood in the frigid darkness, face close to the portal's weathered oak, pulling the thick woollen cape up, close across his face, tugging down on the brim of his black silk hat. Finally, satisfied that he had secured as much protection from the night's privations as could reasonably be achieved, he turned, raised his lantern into the swirling snow and set off along the lane.

Dear God! What a place he had come to. His frozen breath had already rime-crusted the improvised scarf and his numbed feet stumbled over rigid cart tracks and unyielding, icy footprints. The snow had fallen since dawn and now, close to midnight, the narrow way past the church towards the vicarage was knee deep and the hard, cold northerly had cut down from the moor and sculpted a tunnel of high drifts below the sagging, frost encrusted boughs. It was a perverse inverted hell to which the bishop had condemned him and one where he would suffer until the church, or God,

The sexton

believed that he had paid fully and finally for his proclivities.

Oh, one day the winter would end, the snow would melt and even in this forsaken land, the sun might shine; but his heart had drained of warmth that night as they had hurried him past the gallows and sent him north.

As he passed the churchyard his attention was drawn to a pale light between the stones and he paused, glad of the rest from his efforts along the lane, and peered into the night. Surely no honest person could be abroad at such an hour and in such weather as this? He gathered up his cassock and climbed with difficulty onto the bank that surrounded the small cemetery. On the far side a figure toiled beneath a lamp, hung from the lowest branch of an alder. It was the sexton.

'Our Lord in heaven!' Thaddeus scrambled down and waded through the snow, using the tombs as support until he had reached the man and his excavation. 'What is this?' he cried, holding his own light out to better view the scene. 'What in God's name are you about?'

The sexton hardly looked his way, his arms continuing their rhythmic motion: the spade entering the soil, the arms lifting, the blade turning and dropping the dark clod onto the white snow. As the two continued in this way - the one, lantern raised, a look of incredulity on his face, the other his brow wet with perspiration despite the cold, the spade plunging and rising in the frosty ground - the church bell tolled the midnight hour.

Whines & spirits

'They told me of this,' said Thaddeus at last, his features forming into a scowl of distaste, 'how Gideon Pratt foresaw a death and dug the grave before the soul had fled the body! Well, know this, no Christian man can tell what God proscribes, only Satan's spawn would dare to intervene in his great plan! There is no mystery here! I have seen the widow Prescott on her deathbed this very night and I've no doubt that's where you garnered your intelligence. But hear you this! The widow rallies and is expected to overcome her fever! Your claims of prescience owe nothing to devilish consort, more to gossip and a prying eye! Your labour is in vain; your reputation confounded! Do you hear me, Gideon?' And even as he spoke, he knew his own hypocrisy and he shivered at the reminder of how the Prince of Darkness had entered his own soul.

But the sexton never lost his stroke; the black earth heaved from the black recess of the grave to sully the white blanket of snow for a while before it too was slowly lost beneath the ceaseless fall from the invisible sky.

After a while, the parson left and returned to his house where he took a late supper and tried to sleep but the memory of the sexton and that other memory of his own sin, allowed him no rest and at length he took up his cape and hat and he stepped back into the night world.

The snow had stopped at last; the sharp, bright stars were revealed behind the scudding clouds and a silver disc of moon threw reflected light across the silent ice-blue landscape.

The sexton

When the priest reached the grave the sexton had gone, his work complete and a blank, featureless oblong marked the untrodden white expanse. The priest stood and stared into the un-viewable depths and thought on the actions which had brought him to this place and a single tear ran across his cheek and froze into a crystal moon, which reflected the real moon above.

Just before dawn, when the skies had filled with a bank of purple clouds and a few flakes of new snow were drifting across the churchyard, the sexton took the frozen body of Thaddeus McClaver and lowered it gently into the new grave.

You can find a list of other titles
by John A Connor
On page iii of this book

Printed in Great Britain
by Amazon